Please be nice.

"I cannot tell you the meaning of life, but I can tell you how to give your life meaning".

Contents

Prologue

Celtic twilight

I was woken by Cara turning over beneath the bearskin that covered us and our cousins.

"Oh", she sighed, "It's not even beginning to be dawn and mother and the aunts are already up and about".

I was floating in that happy land between dreams and waking and did not want to move, but I knew that I could not hold myself there for long. I opened my eyes just enough to see the shapes moving around the fire and the woodsmoke hanging above me in the almost still air.

I knew that my mother and the aunts were poking the embers of the ever-burning hearth in the centre of our great roundhouse, carefully nurturing the red coals with fresh dry wood from the store under the overhanging eaves as they had done every morning that I could remember. One of them began to add the ingredients stored in the dark angular jars to the mixture in the great cauldron that hung on its iron tripod over the fire – the fat hen, the dry wild mushrooms and lots and lots of Emmer wheat.

When the soup was boiling noisily around the red-hot stones my mother came over and whipped the heavy skin off us, causing a swirl in the smoke and breaking the spell.

“Up” she said, “the dawning soup is doing very well and the day’s work waits to be done”.

I rolled onto my back and stretched slowly, pushing against the others as they also returned from their dreams with equal reluctance. Cara moved over and we both sat up. Reaching behind her she picked up her purplish woollen dress and pulled it over her head. I did the same with my tunic and stood to slip into my trousers. Soon the whole family was up and doing; aunts and uncles, nephews and nieces, cousins and second cousins, and over by the door my Grandfather, the family patriarch, Bran the Elder, after whom I was named. In this way also we were different from our neighbours, where the matriarchs had the last word.

We, all of the children, scampered out of the hut, pushing and laughing, and headed for the gate so that we could go and relieve ourselves on the eastern slopes. That ritual completed, we headed back for our breakfast of hot stew and fresh flat breads.

The meal was soon done, and Cara and I were about to set off to begin our daily tasks when I felt my mother’s arms close around me.

“You, my beautiful boy, need that wild fringe of yours cutting before you walk into a pit for lack of being able to see!”

“Oh mum”, I replied, “but I like it like this. All the warriors have long hair”.

"And when you are a warrior, you can too, but that will be a few years yet so sit still so I don't make a mistake".

I knew I wasn't going to win, because I never did, so I sat still whilst my mother carefully cut away the offending part of my fringe. When she was done, we were glad to leave the smoky darkness of the crowded dwelling. Big as it was, it soon became annoying, filled with the many babies of this spring and the surviving babies of the last, before the entire family moved outside for the day.

We went our separate ways after we had scraped out our bowls into the stinky midden. I walked through the village taking care not to tread on the scattered domes of the clay sealed grain pits, or to disturb any of the dogs stretched out near their owner's huts. One of the domes had already cracked and was giving off the yeasty odour that so pleased the young warriors. I sidestepped a litter of squabbling piglets as I came up to the inner rampart and ran up the bank of the causeway. I stopped to watch the squad of men whose task was to repair the timber box that reinforced our defences, before stretching up to grab the sharpened points of the palisade, pleased that I could finally reach! I pulled myself up until I could see over, scrabbling against the rough bark. The sun was just clear of the curve of the gently swelling downs across the vale. The mist rising from the two winding rivers twisted around the lower slopes that curved away to my left and right, dark and green with their fringe of trees. Through the dips and valleys stretching into the distance, the sea rose like a blue wall underlining the dawn sky. I took a deep breath of the cool damp morning air and with a sigh lowered myself to the causeway and turned to walk around the ramparts to the north side, this being by far the easiest way to cross the crowded random hillfort.

At eleven summers, I was too young for the Warrior Corps. My training with spear and sword would begin next spring to complete my preparation for my manhood feast the summer after, but for now I was a mudlark, a stone picker, a pounder of clay for the potters. I enjoyed that. I liked the feel of the smooth mud squelching through my fingers and I was with my friends.

Moments later I was there, squatting in my usual position beside the pits filled with the dark clay that had been cut from the riverbed far below and carried by the potters' women in wicker baskets up the shallow slopes to the west. The potters' task was never ending since the cordoned brittle pots often broke, ending their useful lives in the waste pits and ditches and littering the steep slopes to the south and west.

I began to pound the lump of clay that had been dumped before me. I punched the clay and folded it over and carefully picked out the stones, grass and bits of shell. The rhythmic pounding quietened my mind, and I did not notice the passing time or the bustle of the village around me, living instead the story that my Grandfather had told us the day before as we sat around the stoked-up fire. Eventually the potter came over to check my work; "Good" was all he said, which was pretty much all he ever said, to us anyway. I exchanged a little smile with my friends and kept on going.

Next time he came to me, he took the clay out of my hands and I sat back to watch him as he deftly rolled the clay into coils and swiftly built up the smooth sides and shaped the rounded lip of the rim. The job complete, he placed the pot on a flat stone, protected from the unpredictable weather by a lean-to supported by four posts, to dry out before firing. Nearby the domed kilns with their stumpy chimneys and long entrance tunnels threw up their plumes of smutty greyish charcoal smoke. Next to the kilns yesterday's firings were spread on the ground and a number of the village women were looking them over. In their hands they carried the lengths of woollen cloth or joints of meat that they would exchange for the items they chose.

The sun was now high in the burnished sky and my thoughts turned to food. I stood, stretching out my cramped muscles, and made my way back around the rampart until I was close to the hut of my family. The midday food was laid out under the eaves and it made my mouth water – flat bread baked in our clay oven, goat's cheese from the herd my brothers shepherded, nuts and berries gathered that morning by Cara and the other girls; thick black sausages with great lumps of fat bound by pig gut and today a rare treat, a handful of oysters gathered by a band of warriors who had weaved between the neighbouring communities to get down to the estuary between the long white cliffs where one of the rivers meandered slowly in to the waiting sea. Eagerly, I took my knife from my belt and set to. I knew only to take what I needed and ate it off the bread, before I ate that also. Washing it down with the flat yeasty ale poured into my upturned mouth from the large jug in my mother's hands.

The afternoon was mine and my friends to spend as we chose, since it was not our turn to tend the flocks or help with the endless repairs, so we decided to go down to the river to swim, and maybe catch some fish. The others didn't bother us much anymore, so long as we stayed out of their fields and didn't stray too close to their enclosures.

Soon we were in the cool water, racing up and down, splashing about and trying to push each other's heads under the water, so laden with clay that you could not see your hand a finger's length in. There was a place on the bank where a tree hung over the water and we took in turns to goad each other into jumping from the thick branches. It felt good flying through the air and crashing into the eddying flow below.

After a while we had finished with our games so we pulled our clothes on and set off back up the hill, pushing each other as we went and trying to make-up insults that we could use when we were old enough to fight.

It was a perfect day, ending as it did with my Grandfather telling us a story, as he so often did. This time it was one of my favourites, the one about the Wolf, the Goat, the Wheatsheaf and the Master who was full of himself.

He settled himself in his usual place and sat smiling into the flames. My Father brought him a bowl of ale, which he took with a smile, and then he began. His voice always melodic and tinged with a half-hidden smile.

"Nearby, and not so very long ago", he began", A clever man was made by things he could not control to work for a Chief chosen not by merit but by birth, which is a strange idea. He often thought to himself that he had never worked out why he was asked every other day, to take a wolf, a goat and a wheatsheaf from his master's land on the left side of the river to his house on the right and then to bring them back on the days in between.

We all know that the raft would only hold one of the others plus him and that wolves eat goats and goats eat wheat, so he had to be careful about the combinations that he left on each bank. He only lost one goat before he worked it out, but that was a long time ago and now it was all feeling a bit pointless.

His wife thought that he was just trying to keep him busy so that he didn't notice how big his hut was compared to theirs, but you know what, he had, and he didn't really care.

So, there he was on the day in question, about to go through the usual routine of taking over the goat and going back empty, then taking over the wheatsheaf and bringing back the goat, then taking over the wolf and going back empty to pick up the hungry goat when HE actually turns up. The master, in person, with a group of his master friends. Seems like he had issued some sort of challenge that they can't work out how to get all three over the river without losing one of the "items".

Anyway, he's brought a long a few spare goats and cabbages (you only ever need one wolf) so off they go and, as you might expect given who his friends are, the goat / wheatsheaf-getting-eaten rate is fairly high, and no-one actually manages to get all three across when the master decides that HE is going to demonstrate!

So, HE gets on the raft with the goat and sets off for the far bank. The goat has a glint in its eye, but nothing happens, and they make it. Back he comes to pick up the wolf , which is the right thing, but now it gets a bit odd because the wolf, un-be-knowns to anyone else but the servant, has been nibbling at the wheatsheaf. He kicks it over to hide the damage and quickly removes a stray stalk from the wolf's impressive incisors but, honestly, he had no idea what was going to happen next.

The master lands, goes over to the wolf and leads it onto the raft. They settle, with the wolf behind the master and set off. Then, halfway across, there is a sudden flurry and the master, headless, is slumped over his oar. The wolf is swimming towards the goat, who helps him out of the water, and off they go into the happy-ever-after. The masters run off screaming leaving the servant and his family with a lot of wheatsheaves".

Grandad's stories always kept me bright-eyed and quiet, but this was my favourite. He always ended by asking us questions and mostly looked to me for an answer first.

"So", he said with half smile looking the other way, "what can we learn from the story of the Wolf, the Goat and the Wheatsheaf?"

I knew he was teasing me by looking away, so I sprung up and jumped in front of him".

"Ah, so Bran has something to say I see. Go on then boy, share your thoughts with us".

I knew that there were several answers that were correct, but I liked the more difficult one.

"Always expect the unexpected, for in life there will be friends who should be enemies and enemies who should be friends … and … never sit with your back to a wolf!"

At that last bit all of the other children laughed. My Grandad stood and messed up my hair before sending us all off to bed.

Chapter 1

Attack on the Caburn

And that was how my life flowed as the seasons turned one upon another but then, when the Romans came, our lives changed forever.

It was a hot day in the early part of summer. I was thirteen years old. Still slight in my boyhood. My fringe though had been allowed to grow out in preparation. This honour was granted to me because of an incident one day when my friends and I had been swimming, as we so often did.

We were returning from the pool in the river when we came across a band of young men from the fort across the vale. Not warriors true, but bigger and older than us. They blocked our way through the woods, and I knew that there was going to be trouble.

"Let us pass", I shouted, wishing that my voice was deeper, "we mean no harm".

"You may not mean harm, but by being here you are doing harm". This from a rangy youth with bad teeth and a wild look in his eyes. "This is our land. You should not be here".

"I was born here", I replied, "and so was my Father, and his Father before him. How long does it take to belong?" I could hear the stress in my own voice and had to make an effort to keep myself strong. The other boys were a step behind me and said nothing, seeming smaller than they had been when we were playing before.

"There is no length of time that could pass that would make you one of us. Go back, you are not welcome here".

I could see in their eyes that nothing I could say was going to make any difference. A long moment passed before, as one, my friends and I leapt forward, dipping to the left and right, in an attempt to get through before these taunting bullies could catch us. I did, being slight and quick, but two of my friends did not and were left struggling in the many arms that held them.

We were running when I realised. Turning I saw one punch land, and then another, and then a kick.

"We must go back", I said, "we cannot leave them". The others looked at me and we could all see the fear we all felt. "Come on".

And with that we did what we knew we should and ran back towards our enemies. They were taken by surprise, focused as they were on their cruelty, and the one who had spoken cried out as I jumped on his back and punched him hard in the ear. The fight was short, since we were only worried about rescuing our friends, and soon we were running together up the clear slopes, leaving those others in a tumble, partly hurting and partly embarrassed.

When were safe within the gates, we broke up and went to our own hearth's. The others must have told the story in a way to make me the leader, although I did not, and it was because of that that I was given the right to grow my hair by the Elders and given the gift of a new dagger from the Druids themselves.

My family had lived here for four generations. I knew that our people had all arrived together. Before that the Isle of Wight was our home. The reasons for moving were not well known but my father had told me that we had been driven from our former homes because of jealousy and greed. My mother told me that we had been made to leave because of our belief in the Gods of the Great Woods and the Moon-Mother. They sometimes spoke with fondness of their imagined past, but by now, of course, there was no-one living here who had even been there. This was our home, My birthplace.

The strong ramparts of our hillfort dominated the valley. The earth banks heaped over the timber box frames and topped with a high wall of stakes kept us safe and as long as we stayed inside it and avoided the fields and lands of our hostile neighbours when we were out, neither man nor beast would do us any real harm. Killing amongst our peoples was rare and children, whichever village they came from, were never hurt. Or so we had always believed.

Now I stood on the walkway behind the main bank and looked down at the massed army below us. Not our usual enemies. These were the Romans. There had been no warning of their coming. No beacons in the east. A sure sign that they had passed through friendly lands. It was only to us that they meant trouble. I could make out our neighbours standing under the shades of the trees, waiting no doubt for the Romans to take the revenge, on their behalf, that they themselves had not been willing to try.

The squares in which they moved looked alien in our wild landscape where all was curves and wild swirls. They had appeared just after dawn. Marching in tight formations to the sound of martial drums. Now they stood in silence. They were not making a camp. I did not think they meant to stay.

Our fort was a beehive of activity. The warriors were preparing themselves for the battle ahead, edging their blades, braiding their hair and painting each other with the signs of honour. Our Druids had a brought a great cauldron out into the open gathering space and the warriors were taking great gulps of the steaming aromatic liquid that fizzed within it.

Our mothers were gathering the young children and taking them to the huts furthest from the gates but I, in between child and man, was left alone to watch the scenes below.

When it came, the sound of their trumpets jarred, making me jump then wonder as the eerie after-sound echoed around the low hills. The sun reflecting off their metal armour, like bolts of lightning, dazzled me and made me squint and half look away, but only half and only for a moment. The squares below seemed to move and breathe as one. The shapes seemed to almost shrug the earth off as they tightened and stood and rows of spearpoints appeared on the sides facing us. Their Leaders rode between them on white horses far bigger than any I had ever seen. The rider's helmets made them seem like giants and carried plumes of bright colours, and then the drums began. Slow and rhythmic, like a storm approaching, and yet the army did not move forward.

I watched our men ride out of the wide-open gate, which looked for the first time small and unfit for its purpose, whereas only yesterday it had seemed a symbol of strength and security. After a long moment I saw the flimsy wicker chariots, in which our battles were always fought, come bouncing across the rutted hillside as they careered down the steep slopes, their drivers whooping and yelling with their spears held high in one hand and the reins gripped loosely in the other as they gloried in their skill.

The mass of Romans swelled slightly but otherwise did not seem to move and, for the first of many times, I felt a sick pain at the base of my stomach. Our men hurtled back and forth in front of the faceless enemy, turning so sharply at each end of the field that one wheel rode up precariously high. I could hear their bellowed insults floating up to me and I thought then what point was there in this when the people you fought did not even speak your tongue.

The Druids dismounted and walked on the balls of their feet right up to the first cohort. Naked, their bodies blazed with swirling woad. I knew from dances and festivals that their eyes would be wide and red and their tongues blue. They raised their trinket laden arms, ready to tell of our previous victories and to curse their foes, their ancestors and descendants in florid and terrifying ways.

They fell together.

Each pierced by a long spear pushed hard between the shield wall, and the Roman mass barely moved. Enraged, the warriors now dismounted and their horses, frightened by the drums, scattered across the lower slopes with the chariots dragging forlornly behind them, many already overturned and breaking up.

Swords drawn and swinging, and spears raised, our brave men ran into the steady ranks, which seemed to tighten in some way the moment before the first impact. I saw the recoil, like a wave struck back by a sheer cliff. I heard the strike of iron on blade and armour. At first many but within minutes just some, then one, then none. Our men lay broken and torn on the grass at the feet of our faceless Roman enemies.

A deep drum, much bigger than the others, began to resonate across the valley. There was a stirring in the woodland. I could see the tops of trees jerking, and a vast animal, unlike anything I had ever seen, slowly emerged into the battle-bright light. Grey and ponderous, it passed between the soldier's square formations. Many men armed with spears and bows rode in a fort on its back. Stretching down from the square power of its head, a long limb swung before it between two great tusks. The sickness in my stomach turned to cold fear as the beast began its steady climb towards our gate, which suddenly looked even smaller and more feeble. Just one square of troops broke position and began to follow in its giant footsteps. The others turned as one and moved on. The space they left behind littered with our twisted dead. It seems that those of us who were left were not worthy of their full force.

I sprinted across to the gate, and with the old men and other boys rushed to close it and bar it as best we could, grabbing any timbers, jars or anything else we could lift, to try and give it more of a chance against the power of the beast. Even so, our gate lasted almost no time at all. At first, we tried to hold it as the ropes frayed and the timbers split, but we knew there was no hope.

So then we set fire to it to try and stop the creature or, at least, to buy ourselves some time. Its massive head pushed the final timbers cracked and the gate went down amidst screams and cries of bitter anguish. Like a rolling rock, it stepped over the debris and the Romans followed through.

Silent, grim, relentless.

One old man stood proud before them. He was pushed aside and left where he fell. One boy, my friend Annan with whom I had been playing at the river only a few days ago, took a spear and ran to attack the leading soldiers, but one of them just struck him a glancing blow, took the spear off him and pushed him out of the way. We all knew in that chilling moment that the two things that we could do were bend the knee and pray; or run.

Our men lay dead in the valley below. Our defences were broken. The presence of the war-beast terrified us. We knelt, made prisoners by our own barricades and the steep slopes beyond them.

The soldiers spread like a stream of blood through the roundhouses, a mix of bronzed and dark-skinned men unlike any I had ever seen. They brought the leather and rope with which to bind us. They pushed us roughly into two long lines and joined us at the neck with loose nooses secured to long poles, our hands tied behind us. I had no time to reach our hut to find my family and I could not see them in the panicking crowd.

We were taken from the barricade in those untidy lines. Crossing through our village for the last time, we were led out of the smouldering gate and down the slope into the deep shadows under the trees below and whatever dark future lay before us.

As we went, the others poured in. Men, women and children

from the surrounding settlements who had traded with us and sometimes eaten with us but who always resented our possession of the Caburn. They would now sleep in our beds, warm themselves at our hearths and eat the meat from our herds. But they would not find the offerings hidden in the sacred heart of the village. They at least would be safe.

Our path took us across the field of combat. Our druids looked foolish, spiked like codfish. Our warriors lay where they had fallen. Their swords bent and broken on the Roman iron, so much harder than our own.

My brother lay there, his dark hair soaked with blood. His bright eyes dull and cold. My father also, frozen and empty where once had lodged such energy and love. I turned away and tears filled my eyes. My stomach cramped and I tried to bend to be sick, but I was held in place by the noose and my vomit spilled onto my chest.

In that most awful of moments, I resolved that I would not give in. The sight of their bodies lit a cold flame that would burn in my heart until I had, in some way, in any way, taken my revenge. I didn't realise, in my youth, that such feelings were common, but the revenge was rarely achieved.

But first I must find out if my mother lived, and my sisters and my little brothers. Everything had happened so quickly that I had had no time to find them and protect them as best I could. The attack had been like an avalanche. Irresistible. Inevitable. All absorbing and in my terror, I had lost them. At first, I could not make them out in the bleak huddles of my people. The dreadful events of the day had seemed to fade us all.

But then I saw them, and my heart leapt in my chest. My mother to my left with the other women. Tied at the ankles, her long hair unbraided and tangled. Her face stained with tears. My brothers in another group, huddling together, tied wrist to wrist, looking around with fearful darting eyes. They saw me and tried to jump up, only to fall together when their tied ankles tripped them. Only my sisters were missing now. I scanned the bound groups beneath the trees looking for their familiar bright clothing, but they were not there. I did not know then that I would never see them again.

As much as I wanted to, I could not go to my mother or my brothers, bound as I was, and so we spent that first evening starring at each other in turn, trying to will what comfort we could into our frightened eyes. The clear sky sucked the heat out of us as the sun set, and the chill sank deeper into us when we saw the fires of our hearths springing up on the hill above us and knew that they were warming the limbs of those amongst whom we had lived for so long, but of whom we had never truly been a part.

I suppose I must have slept. My arms and legs were numb and there was a sharp pain in my left hip. My first instinct was to seek out my mother and my breathing calmed when I saw her shape across the way. Now the hill was framed by a faint glow and the ten thousand stars were brilliant. The valley was dark in the absence of the Moon-Mother. I sensed a movement and felt the touch of a hand on my shoulder, causing me to start up and then freeze. Whoever it was put their mouth to my ear and in the faintest whisper of warm breath laid out for me my destiny, lying there in the black night amongst the fallen and the imprisoned.

"We must not let the unbelievers take the treasures of the Great Gods. You must go for them. Save them. Take them to the far west. Take them to the safe haven in the cave at the end of time. Deep in the slate mountain where only the faithful will find them. You must make the six nine".

I did not understand that last phrase, but the meaning of the rest of the words sank in and I felt the sick grip of fear in my tummy. I wanted to stay close to my mother and my brothers and this disembodied voice was telling me that I could not.

"But how will I do this. The Romans are here around us and our fort is occupied by the Others".

'There is a way. Beneath the east rampart where the land falls quickly into the rough gorse there is a hidden entrance. You might think it a badger set from the look of it, but it quickly widens. The passage will take you up into the rampart itself where you will find a small chamber. There, by feeling around the walls, you will touch a wooden panel secured with iron pins. You will need to pull them out, but only when you have listened to make sure the other side is quiet. When the panel is removed you will see the roots of turf, for the covering there is thin. From the outside there is no join to see. Cut the turf with the knife that you will find there. Make two cuts across each other so that the hole you leave will be less clear. Push through and let the turf fall back into place behind you. Once inside you will be close to the sacred pit at the centre of our Druid Shrine. I left the offerings near to the surface in the hope that I would be able to get them. I could not, so now, you must".

Now I knew who I was talking to. It was Elder Druid so I knew that I could not refuse.

"Can I bring them back to you?"

"You cannot. That would place them in great danger. You must go west. I will take care of your mother and brothers as best I can".

In that there was some small comfort, at least in my ignorance of the fate of slaves and my belief in the power of the wise man, I thought so then.

"But I am tied".

At once, I felt my bonds loosen and then, without a sound, the last Druid was gone, back to the other old men.

It was only later that I learned that old men were of no value to the Romans and that, at best, they would be left behind and of no use to my family. Had we known he could have waited whilst I stole into the Sanctuary and undertaken the journey himself. But we did not know.

It was not that I didn't have a choice. I could have stayed where I was and done what I could to protect my mother and my brothers and search for my sisters, but to have done so would have been a betrayal of my oaths, taken at twelve, to protect the Gods first and above all else. I flexed my wrists and ankles and slowly rolled onto my side. My eyes were good in the dark and I could see that the guards around us were well spaced out and slumped in that half sleep that boredom, complacency and darkness can bring on.

The largest gap was to my left and so I began to edge that way. At first my movements were almost imperceptible. I didn't want to wake the other boys or give the guards reason to stir, but soon a gap appeared between me and the other prisoners and my intention would have been clear to any guard alert enough to see me.

It was my good fortune that none of them were and, after what seemed an age of slow and careful movement, I was beyond the perimeter of slumbering troops and able to move more quickly.

As the ground rose towards the summit the trees and undergrowth thinned. I kept low so as not to break the skyline for any who might be looking up from below and hoped that any sound I made would be taken for a fox, wolf or even a wild boar, all of which were common here. The flints were cruelly sharp beneath my hands and knees and I could fell trickles of hot blood running down my legs.

Soon, I was looking down on the banked fires of the slumbering camp and able to move more freely. The slope here was steep but

I had been climbing up and down it since I was old enough to leave my mother's side and I knew which paths to take.

I made my way crabwise at an angle and soon found myself below the east rampart. There were several patches of tough gorse clinging to the slope and it was not until I had fruitlessly explored two that I came across the dark, forbidding hole that, as the Druid had said it would, could easily have been taken for a badger set. Small though I was I had to discard my cloak and belt before I could push myself into the darkness, trusting in the words of the Elder that I would not become jammed amidst the sharp flints. I had to make more than one attempt, finally managing it by putting one arm in first and pushing hard with my left foot against a gnarled old root. Once my shoulders were through the rest was easy enough. Inside the hole did widen quickly, so much so that I was able to turn and reach out and pull in my cloak and belt.

I sat awhile, crouched in the darkness, waiting for my eyes to be able to pick up any light there may have been, but there was none. Some crawling insect fell on to my face and I banged my head in the act of brushing it off. I stilled my breath and listened for any sounds of other movement, but I could hear nothing. After what seemed an age I shuffled around on to my hands and knees and began to crawl further into the blackness. I had to put one hand in front of me to avoid banging my head on the low roof, armed as it was with sharp flint, but there was no saving my knees. I could feel that the tunnel was rising and knew from my explorations of the fort that I could not be more than thirty feet from the inside of the rampart. It seemed an age before I entered a wider chamber and, working around its rooted walls, I touched the hard wood of the panel. I felt around and found the iron pins that were tightly fixed in the chalk. I stopped my breathing again and listened, my ear pressed against the hidden door. I could hear nothing and so, one at a time, I slowly eased each pin out of position, using my other hand and my forehead to stop the panel falling away. When it was free, I eased it out and lowered it to the stony floor. I listened again and, again, I heard nothing, so I took my blade from its sheath and carefully pushed it through the close bound roots. I felt the point slip through and gently sawed down and across for the length of my forearm. The first cut completed, I began on the second and soon a gap appeared. I stopped and put my left eye close to it. In the faint light I could see that there was no-one moving so I finished the cut, sheathed my knife, and carefully pushed the triangles of turf away from me. The hole was just big enough for me to pull myself through, emerging like a mole, and soon I was crouching on the turf of my former home, wide-eyed and frightened but certain of what I must do.

I crept through the shadows of the low roundhouses and made my way towards the shrine. The new owners of our village had no thought of posting guards on this night; with the Romans below they felt no need, and so the task was made a little easier.

The Gods house was bigger than those around it and marked by the horned skulls on each of the door posts. That side was still well lit, and I was forced to enter by another way. I flattened myself to the ground and rolled under the dark eves of the thatch. The woven wall itself was lined on my side with clay pots and I knew that I would have to move at least one and maybe two to get through, even though I knew that in them floated the severed heads of our slain enemies. They were sealed with leather skins tied tightly in place, their empty eyes staring in an endless darkness, and I was careful not to dislodge the coverings. I had no wish to see the dead within, or for their spirits to get a glimpse of me. It was only the permission of the Elder to be here that gave me the courage to pull two of them carefully aside. That done, the wattle panel was easily prised apart with the aid of my knife. This most holy of places did not need strong walls for normally none but the Druids would dare approach it.

The air was thick with hemp smoke which curled and twisted around the inscribed stone at the centre of the fearful space. I crept forward and pushed against the lid, for such it was, of the sacred pit. At first it resisted but then it suddenly gave and moved quickly aside and beneath it I could see the shape of sacred gold. I lifted out the three torcs, each wrapped in fine woven cloth, and placed them in my shoulder bag. Once this was done, I silently dragged the stone back into place, leaving some small items in the pit. A brooch, a comb, some fragments of bone. My hope was that, when their Druids had finished with their spells and incantations and were ready to open the shrine, they would find these and think that that was all we had, being poor and isolated, and so not pursue me. I pushed the bag through the hole that I had made and then crawled through myself. I knew that it was important that my removal of the offerings went undetected and so I took my time remaking the wattle until my place of entry was undetectable. I last replaced the jars with their gruesome contents, apologising to the warriors within for my rudeness in disturbing them.

The camp was even quieter now and I was able to swiftly make my way back to the hidden entrance to the tunnel through the chalk. I pushed my feet through first, if anyone had been watching it would have seemed as if the earth itself was sucking me in. Again, I took as long as I needed to align the turf and re-pin the panel before crawling downward through the steeply sloping confines of the tunnel and out into the moonless night.

I knew that I must go, but still I sat staring down into the valley where my mother and my brothers were bound and frightened and where the bodies of my father and my older brother lay where they would be left to rot. I wanted to go down and hand my burden to another and stay with my family, but I knew that I could not and so I cried and rocked and held myself until my tears went dry and then I knew it was the time. My way was clear now, and it was not theirs.

Chapter 2

The escape

I made my way around the curved slopes of the middle of the hill to the long ridge behind. It was now the darkest part of the night which made me safer from the Romans and their allies but put me at risk from the big animals and fast packs that roamed outside our barricades. The flickering glow of the smouldering gate was the only illumination. I decided to stay on the high ground where the trees were sparse and the undergrowth patchy so that I would have time to react if anything were to charge at me.

My first steps took me to the north and west. I knew this way well from hunting with my father and the others in the few months since I had turned thirteen. Going north first was the only way that made any sense, and to then go west because the rivers were too wide and deep to cross without the services of a boatman as they approached the sea. Thoughts of my family made my feet drag and stick but I knew that I must go on, even though the pain of my losses since the Romans came made tears flow freely down my face again, as they would most days when I woke and in the hours before sleep.

Before long the land began to drop away, and features were picked out by the first darting beams of the new sun rising behind the downs and slicing through the cool mist in the valleys. As the landscape opened before me, I made better time and I was soon far enough away from the Roman camp to be sure that I could stop and rest. To be safe I crawled into a clump of gorse, following a narrow path created by some roaming animal, most likely wild boars, then pushed some branches aside to make a small clearing, and there I lay upon my cloak with my dagger in my hand and closed my eyes.

My dreams brought me no comfort, filled as they were with the cries of the dying and the tears of those left behind, and I woke stiff and shivering, after only a brief sleep, in the light of early morning. Once free of my sheltering gorse I took a moment to look around. There was no movement on the high places, and I assumed that my escape had either gone unnoticed or been ignored. I was one boy among many, and none had bothered to count us.

The valleys below were still filled with the drifting mists of dawn and so were places of danger and to be avoided. I had woken hungry and had to eat and drink, but I had nothing with me. The bushes though were rich in nuts and berries and I would find a dewpond soon enough, so I set my bag on my shoulder and set off, keeping the sun to my back and my right so that I knew that I was heading inland and north, grazing as I went. Sure enough, I soon found a shallow pond, drank till my thirst was gone and filled the leather flask that always hung at my belt, to see me through.

The sun was still low when I came to the first river. Where our paths crossed it was still deep and wide and I could not cross in safety. Turning right I began to follow the bank. I expected to come across family settlements and even small villages on the water's edge but that held no fear for me. It was only our close neighbours who envied our high position and resented our presence, even only this far away I knew that I could expect the hospitality extended to travellers by rote and rule.

Even so, on the first day of my journey when I came upon two small hamlets, each with three or four huts but wide paths stretched away from each of them into the woods speaking to me of connections and shared ways I was wary. I did not want any contact with people who might have friends or family amongst those who had proven to be our enemies and so I passed them by and journeyed on.

But the next day, I did better. Within the first hour of walking, I came across a settlement that might suit. A small collection of huts on top of a high bank. Crouching in the woodland I could see that one of them was the living space and the others were for livestock and a few tools. The door covering was pulled back, so I knew that the inhabitants were up. An older man came out, stretched, and made his way into the woods behind the house, no doubt to do his morning business away from the settlement. A woman followed, not so old but old enough to be grey. She went over to the open fire in the middle of the clearing. A cauldron hung from a tripod above it, its contents steaming in the cool morning air. She dropped in some greens that she had been carrying, then went across to a growing patch and plucked some leaves from the herbs that were thriving there. These too were added to the thick vegetable stew that I knew would be in the pot. An inquisitive goat had come too close and it earned a swift slap on its nose to drive it away. The man returned and settled next to the fire. The woman put her hand on his shoulder, and he covered it with his own for a moment.

There was a stirring at the door and two more members of the community emerged. A long-haired girl of about my age and a smaller boy who I placed around nine or ten. They also disappeared briefly into the woods before coming and sitting with the man. If I was to share their breakfast, now was the time to make myself known. I stood, moved forward to the edge of the clearing and waited, as custom dictated, to be acknowledged and invited in. The four of them were stilled by my appearance. All of their heads were pointed my way and I could almost feel their gaze and their curiosity. These parts were well populated but even so, people did not move between settlements without purpose, and then it was mostly bands of hunters or women trading. Eventually the man spoke.

"Come, friend, join us in our morning food". He spoke slowly and with warmth.

"Thank you, Sir", I replied, touching my chest over my heart.

"A blessing on you and your family for your kindness this day".

The formalities dealt with, I joined them on the logs around the cauldron. The woman handed me a flat, black pottery bowl into which she had ladled a generous helping of the steaming pottage. For a while we ate in silence, then the man spoke again.

"You must have travelled through the night to reach us at this early time? Or come from close by".

"Both are true Sir". I knew that I must tell him the truth. To do otherwise, in light of my welcome would have been wrong. "I have come from the Caburn".

There was no bristling at my words, no unconscious straightening, only a pause and an exchange of glances. The girl touched the man's arm, asking his permission to speak this first time. He put his hand on hers in confirmation. Her voice was light but tinged with concern.

"We were on the near hill and saw smoke from that way two nights ago. More than cooking fire would make, and there are no feast days close".

"Was there a battle?" the boy broke in, clearly excited by the images that thought brought to mind. The man shot him a glance that silenced him and made him lower his head into his shoulders.

"You must forgive him. We have few visitors here".

I smiled, being still young enough to remember making such mistakes myself.

"There was a battle, but it was not like any battle that we have seen before. The Druids were slain before the chanting had barely begun. There was no exchange of insults or tales of victories gone. The enemies were faceless and still, like a grey rock, until our warriors struck and then, in moments, fell to single thrusts from the solid wall of shields. It was not an honourable victory".

"They have been before", the old man said", in the time of my grandfather's grandfather, "then also there was little dignity or honour. They fought as one and had great beasts with forts upon their backs. Moving hills with tusks many times the size of any boar. My father told me the stories. They took many slaves and much other tribute then sailed back across the narrow sea. If they are back, then dark times are ahead of us".

"There was such a beast. As high as three men and the size of many cattle. After our men were killed, they used it to push down our gates. There was no way of stopping it".

For the first time the old woman now spoke, "Husband, do you think we should move away. The first crossing is close, and the invaders may well come this way".

"Bran has spoken of an attack that happened two days ago. The valley runs east to west so it would seem that they have gone a different way, at least for now.

The two children looked first at her and then at him, waiting anxiously. He stared into the fire, took a mouthful of the stew, chewed it slowly, then spoke.

“It is a hard thing, but I think the way is clear. If we stay here and the Romans come our way we will be killed or pushed aside, and the children taken as slaves”. He paused again and the silence thickened, “we must take refuge in the west. The first tribes at least will let us pass, especially if we give them warning, and with luck each battle we put between us and the invaders will make us safer. As the sand slows the incoming waves, so the fight might make the Romans weary and they will think the land they have, is enough”.

“When shall we go, Grandfather?” This time it was the girl who spoke.

He addressed his family. “Bran has travelled only a few short nights, and we have seen the smoke of the Caburn’s gates. If the Romans come this way, or those who would take advantage of chaos they cause. Trouble will find us. If we are going to leave, we must leave now”.

No-one moved as the decision sank in. The boy and girl had known no other place than this. The woman moved first, rising quickly to begin the gathering of that which they could carry. The children now also went to select from their beds the few things that they would take.

The grandfather, who told me now that his name was Macklyn, gathered a few small tools that might be useful. We talked of weapons and decided that his boar spears would be of most use. They would be no threat to armed men that we might meet, and therefore not provoke a response that one old man and a thirteen-year-old boy on the edge of manhood would not be able to counter, but they would provide protection from the roaming herds of wild boar or packs of wolves, or even lone bears, that we might encounter as we moved into the less settled, more desolate lands towards which we were headed.

It was still early in the day when we set off. The last act of the family was to free their goats and remaining chickens, having killed and cooked four of them to sustain us in the first part of our journey. The house they left as it was. Since they had no further use for it, it was customary to leave it for another.

Macklyn knew this area well and, since we believed that the Romans would head west and cross at the lowest possible point, took us due north, following the river's bank until we reached a point shallow enough for us to safely cross. We all quickly removed our sandals and stripped off our clothes. Wet sandals would have been no use on our journey, and we had no time to dry our garments. With everything in bundles balanced on our heads we stepped forward into the dark waters. Within a few steps it was clear that the boy, Galvyn, was too short and so Macklyn took his bundle and I hitched him up onto my back. His slight weight made no difference as I pushed forward through the brown stream, the black mud, which I prayed would get no deeper, oozing between my toes.

We were soon resting on the other bank. Our woollen cloaks dried us and, refreshed with some cold meat, we continued on our way, climbing the gentle slope away from the river. Macklyn told us that it was a day's walk to the edge of the Great Forest that lay in our path, part obstacle, part refuge, for once inside it, it would be almost impossible for the Romans, or any other pursuer, to find or follow us.

It was when we stopped at midday to eat that I learned the true history of my travelling companions. I did not ask. Olwen, as I now knew the old woman to be called, volunteered the information.

"I see Bran that you look at us and wonder at our age, with two children so young, but that you are well mannered and will not ask. Galvyn and Alane are our grandchildren. Their mother was our daughter. She had been with her husband, bound by law and ceremony, for some years. Alane was on her feet and speaking when our daughter fell pregnant with the boy. It was not an easy birth, away as she was from me, in the village of her husband. The boy came after a long labour. Exhausted and torn she became ill with a fever from which she did not recover. They buried her in that far place. We have never seen her grave. Olwen paused there and I could see the grief of her loss in her dark eyes and felt a deep connection growing form our shared experience of loss.

There were no women in the family there who could feed the child or see to its' needs, and so, one day, the father rode into our clearing with a child in each saddle basket and gave them to us, and we were glad to have them.

For a few years he came by with gifts and food, but then we saw him no more. We think he must have died for he was a good man who grieved for our daughter and loved his children. We will never know, there is no-one to tell us".

Through this telling Macklyn sat with his head bowed and the two children sat cross legged on the ground, stared unblinking at their grandmother with their heads supported by their hands.

"I am sorry that your daughter died. My father and brother were killed when the Romans came." Now it was my turn to stop, as the raw pain of my loss caused tears once again to wet my cheeks. "My mother and my other siblings were taken. Not knowing where they are now or how they are faring is hard for me to bear."

Macklyn looked up now. His gaze was steady and calm and even before he spoke, I found his quietness reassuring.

"We are happy that you found us, and honoured that you choose to travel with us, even though we slow you down. We are all family now".

Galvyn smiled, jumped up and came over to sit by me, leaning against my side as my little brothers used to do. A tear escaped me and fled down my cheek. Olwen came across and gently brushed it away. She raised my chin with the same hand and kissed me on my forehead.

After a long moment Macklyn spoke again.

"We must be on our way. These slopes are exposed, and the Romans or their spies may well be looking. They will also realise that they must come inland to go west, although they may have the means to cross where the rivers are wider. We must put more paces between us and them and hope the tribes will slow their progress once they get into the interior and away from the familiar traders of the coast".

With that we gathered our few belongings, cleared the site and scuffed up the grass as best we could to conceal our presence and began to walk again. Macklyn first, then Olwen and Alane in the middle, then Galvyn and then me with one of the boar spears, aware that the rear was the most likely place for any attack, whether it be by Romans, bandits or wolves.

There was little heat in the sun even in the hours after midday. A sure sign that the season was changing. We would need to push on if we were to reach safety before the winds and rains of winter made the way much harder.

We made good time and it was early evening when we sighted the first of the Oaks at the edge of the darkening woods and some hours more before we passed beneath them and into their welcoming shadows.

Chapter 3

Into the forest

The gloom beneath the canopy brought night early as we made our way deeper into the ancient forest. We took care to do no harm as we made our way, careful to be respectful of the spirits that we felt around us.

After we had put a few thousand paces between ourselves and the outside we decided to stop and make a camp for the night. We had left the first oaks far behind and could see none nearby in which we could have found safety in its spreading boughs, so we had to make do with a bed of leaves on the damp ground.

Macklyn went about the business of making a small fire in the lee of a rotten, long fallen trunk. We felt sure that this could not be seen from the forests edge, and yet might still be useful in discouraging predators, of which there might be many near-by.

Galvyn and I agreed to go in search of nuts and berries, and maybe a fungus that we knew, since none of us had either the energy or the inclination to go hunting in the failing light. This would normally have been for Olwen and Alane to do, but we did not judge it safe enough.

Before dawn we would be proven right.

After we had eaten, we wrapped ourselves in our cloaks and lay close together to try and get some sleep. Macklyn was first to guard, my turn would come when he judged the night half done. I fell asleep with a clear image of him sitting on our sheltering tree firmly holding his boar spear, partly for defence, and partly for support.

I do not know how long it had been when he nudged me in the ribs with the shaft. Even half asleep I knew better than to move or make a sound when woken in this way, for it could only mean danger. I lay still but alert, straining to hear any sound that might give me a clue to the cause of Macklin's alarm. Whether it be a bear, a wolf or a wildcat? With luck just a snuffling boar, maybe even one that we could kill and butcher to give us more fresh meat.

At the edge of my vision Macklyn slowly rose to his feet and lowered his spear so that the long iron tip pointed into the darkness. I risked enough movement to be able to look into the undergrowth, even if the darkness made the animal almost impossible to see. I heard a heavy branch being pushed aside, no wildcat then, or wolf. Something large.

The bear moved slowly into our small clearing, sniffing the air before it. Moving its great head slowly from side to side. I had never seen such a beast before, only heard tales of its monstrous size and limb tearing jaws. My spear was next to me but even so I doubted if I would have the strength to hold it against the charge of such a creature.

The fireside tales of my childhood had though given me some helpful knowledge and I knew that once the animal was so close the best thing to do was nothing at all, since we were not its natural prey. I just hoped that the others would not wake and, in their panic and surprise, startle the bear and provoke a swift and surely fatal attack. Bears did not eat the meat of anything that was already dead so if we could lay still it would sniff around then go.

Like a snake the sinuous neck supporting the razor-toothed jaw swayed forward, getting ever closer to the sleeping boy. I tensed, checking from the corner of my eye where my spear was.

Galvyn's first scream pierced the night. No-one could blame him. A man of any age could not be silent if, when opening his eyes, he was confronted with those teeth a hands breadth from his face.

There was no gap in time at all between the scream and the

reaction of his grandfather. Macklyn had clearly already made a plan. He dropped swiftly to his left and dipped his hand into the still hot ashes of our fire and, scooping them up, he threw them into the air in front of the now rearing bear. Galvyn, at the same moment, scuttled backwards into the arms of Olwen who gripped him fiercely, her dagger drawn.

The bear's forward movement took it into the cloud of ash which immediately irritated its eyes and nose causing it to pause, shake its head and run a clawed paw over its nose. Understanding only that whatever it was that was causing it discomfort was in front of it, it twisted away still brushing at its streaming nose, and lumbered back into the woods.

No one moved as it pushed its way back into the gloom. I do not think that Macklyn's trick would have worked twice and even two boar spears in the hands of an old man and a boy would have been of little use in saving us if the bear had struck at Galvyn.

Looking back, I think we were saved by the season. At the end of summer, the bear was fat and lazy. If we had met it after its winter sleep, it might not have been so easy to make it abandon its feast.

For the rest of that night the two children lay in Olwen's arms, wrapped firmly in her loving embrace, and Macklyn and I sat back-to-back scanning the trees for any sign of movement.

Eventually, after what felt like the longest night of my life, the sky began to brighten. I climbed a nearby tree so that I could more carefully note the point on the horizon where it was first pierced by the sun. Keeping that in sight and at our backs would allow us to make sure that the progress we made on our journey was generally to the west and the safety of the mountains that we knew to be there.

No one felt like gathering any berries or nuts in the woods after our encounter with the bear so we ate a few mouthfuls of the precious cold chicken, made up our bundles and set off, this time with me taking the lead and Macklyn at our rear.

The next few days passed without incident as we made our way through the mix of old woods and scrubby heathland. What few signs of settlement we came across we skirted around, not wanting to get involved in the rituals of travellers and hosts, focused as we were on putting as much distance between us and the Romans as we could. I, also, felt the weight of the three torcs in their hiding place around my tummy and was conscious of the need to keep the risk of their discovery as low as possible.

On the third day we came upon a stream and took some time to drink, wash our feet and replenish our water bags. The morning mist drifted in strands across the shallow valley, covering us like a cloak and giving us a sense of safety in the gathering light of day.

Refreshed, we made our way from the gentle bank and back into the dense woodland, always wary but talking loudly so that any creature had time to move away before we intruded on them. Galvyn trotted along beside me asking me an endless stream of questions about my life in the Caburn and about the attackers who had caused me to flee.

I answered him as fully as I was able, even though talking about my life before brought back memories that were both bitter and sweet.

"When I was your age", I said, "I had my list of daily chores to do. My warrior training had yet to begin so I was expected to help with the household tasks. There was no water on the hill".

"Then why did you live there? Would it not have been better to live alongside a river like we did?" He asked, briefly walking backwards in front of me.

"It would have been", I replied, pulling him around so that he faced the direction in which we were going, "except that we were not much liked by the others who lived nearby".

"Why was that?" he said, "I can't see that anyone would not like you".

I smiled and gave him a friendly shove, which made him giggle and try to shove me back.

"My people were not the same as them. In my grandfather's grandfather's time, we had left our home on an island to the west after a falling out caused a blood feud with a dangerous neighbour and come to live in the chalk hills. My father said we brought good iron with us as gifts and, at first, the local people were welcoming. But as time went by those gifts were forgotten and they saw only that we spoke oddly and wore our cloaks pinned differently and used pots that were finer. We all knew that we and were more worshipers of the Moon Mother than their Woodland Gods with their Wicker Men". It was just that we didn't care.

Galvyn's head ducked a little then.

"I have heard of the Wicker Men. My grandparents say that that is one of reasons why we chose to live in the clearing by the river, rather than in a large village".

"I've never seen any of their ceremonies, and from what I have heard, I never want to. We also kept to ourselves, only venturing out to hunt or gather as we needed in those first years. Later things seemed more relaxed and we had uneasy agreements that allowed more freedom, so long as we were respectful. But I do know that, even so, they were in some way afraid of us. They made a guardian on a slope nearby to protect them from us. A huge man standing with two spears made with raised turf banks that appeared when the sun was in the right place to make the turfs cast shadows".

Galvyn looked thoughtful. He had a new question.

"Why did the strangers attack you? You could do them no harm".

"I don't know. Before they appeared in the valley beneath us there was no smoke or any signs of people running before an invader".

"Maybe the others were their friends", said the boy.

"Perhaps they were", I replied, "I had seen ships before sailing in sight of the chalk cliffs. They were trading, I think".

We fell silent and walked on. He a few steps in front of me. It was dusk before we stopped again. After our fright on the night of the bear, we took time to find somewhere much safer to make our camp. Macklyn and Olwen chose the base of a mighty Oak. The roots would shield our small cooking fire from sight. We felt the tree would welcome us making our beds in its spreading branches, safe at least from the larger beasts that roamed these woods.

Macklyn and I followed a boar path into the undergrowth in the hope of some meat but nothing came our way, so we all gathered some greens and berries from the nearest bushes and plants and Olwen made a hot stew in the small iron pot that she carried for that purpose.

A stillness in the clearing, at the middle of which the Oak stood, made us drowsy and it had only been dark a moment before we took to the broad branches and nooks of our lofty camp and settled down for the night. At the last I lay and watched the Moon Mother, full and round and bright hanging in the sky above us, sitting in a bed of clouds whose colours changed as the wind pushed them along. My sleep, for once, was dreamless.

It must have been a sound that woke me. Moon Mother was still high but had moved across the crowded sky, so I knew some part of the night had passed. I raised my head without moving my shoulders and looked around. The sight below me made me freeze, the fear like a stabbing pain in my tummy.

Around us stood nine shrouded figures, none touching but grouped in threes equally spaced to encircle the Oak. Their faces were not visible under the deep hoods. They were still. Each with its hands held low before it. I had never seen them hooded in this way, but I knew who stood around us. Druids.

Those in our camp were advisors to our warriors and to our Chief. Ornate in swirling woad. Pierced in the ears and elsewhere, often naked. Their hair uncut. They spent much of their time tending to the shrine or just sitting, staring, or so it seemed to me as young boy. But I had heard of other Druids. Druids who lived in dark places, who owed no allegiance to any fort or village. Druids who guarded the most sacred places and in a moment of dread I began to wonder if we now found ourselves, through no fault of our own, in such a place.

The cloaked figures began to hum a low steady note. Those in front held it first for a long breath and then the next three picked it up. In this way it moved around us. After each third circuit the note rose both in pitch and volume. Alane was woken first and started up, I put my hand on her arm to still and steady her. Soon the other three were equally alert, bound together by our fear and linked also by one hand upon the next arm.

As the sun broke the horizon the sound suddenly ceased and in one well practised movement, the Druids pulled back their hoods and in doing so revealed their long-braided hair and woven pointed beards. In the stillness of that first contact I took in dense swirls of woad on each of their cheeks and foreheads. Not painted on as was the way with our Druids but drilled in with needles to make then last forever.

After what seemed like an age the Druid to our left spoke in a slow, almost sleep-like way, as if he were only partly of this place, but mostly in some other.

"Who is it that sits now in the branches of the Great Oak? Are you of this world or another?"

Macklyn and I exchanged worried glances, but he showed no sign of answering.

"Speak now".

I could not tell if that had been the same Druid or another. The glade in which the Oak stood was still swathed in the strands of mist which seemed to bend the sound as well as the low sun's light. I felt rather than knew that it was up to me to answer the Druids questions.

"Sir. Elder. We are of this world. We mean no harm. We are travellers running ahead of the Roman invaders and we needed a safe place to rest".

Another Druid spoke.

"We sense more in you than you have shared".

And another.

"Many have passed this way since the Moon Mother's belly was last full".

And another.

"They too have spoken of the Roman's and the grey beasts that they have with them".

And another.

"All are heading to the west to find refuge beyond the twisting rivers that cut the land".
And another.

"But there is more for you to tell us before you pass".

I was thrown into confusion by the different voices all seeming to be from the same mind. I knew that I had no choice but to put my faith in these Mystic Leaders of the Great Woods.

"I have a mission to complete in the west", there was a long pause. I felt the eyes of all my companions as well as the Druids on me. "When the Caburn fell I was captured with the others. But in the darkness our last Druid freed me and gave me instructions and permission and I crept into the dark tunnel and made my way back to our shrine and removed the three torcs that lay there. I have them still."

The central Druid to the front of me took three paces forward.

"Show us".

I took the torcs from their hiding place beneath my ribs. In some sense I felt guilt at not having shared them with my new family before, but it had seemed best to keep the presence of these sacred objects to myself, in case one of us had been taken.

"All nine of the Druids moved around to form a loose semi-circle in front of us. The torcs glowed in the dawn light, as only gold can do. No-one spoke for an uncomfortably long time. It was the Druid who had spoken first who broke the silence.

"Come down brother. You and your family will be safe with us".

I carefully wrapped the torcs in the soft cloth, making sure that they did not touch as I had been told, and then we all helped each other to clamber down out of the branches where we had taken sanctuary.

The Druids took up positions around us, forming a shape that may have been an eye or a boat, and then we moved quickly and quietly into the trees.

It was only a short walk to their enclosure. Approached down a narrow path through dense and uninviting bushes, the entrance was bound by two thick posts on which ancient symbols of defiance and defence had been carved. They were similar to those I had seen on the much smaller posts of our shrine, but these were more finely carved and ornate.

Once we were through the formation broke up and most of the Druids worked together to lift a solid wooden screen into the gap and secure it with cross beams and some angled posts that slotted into grooves in the back. That completed the circular boundary of sharpened logs, all of which were almost twice the height of a tall man.

Inside the enclosure there were four roundhouses, three equally distributed around the outer circle, and one, larger and taller, in the dead centre.

One of the Druids turned to me and held out his hands.

"Give me the torcs friend".

I hesitated, feeling the heavy weight of my responsibility. He seemed to be able to read my thoughts, or maybe just sense my concern.

"They will be safe. I will place them in the centre of the shrine, which you see here before you, and no one will touch them again until they are returned to you when you go on your way".

I knew that to question the word of a Druid would be absurd and so I handed him the precious bundle. I was surprised how relieved I suddenly felt not to have them concealed about me for a while.

Gentle hands guided us into the smoky interior of the first hut to the left of the entrance where we were pleased to see a spread of comfortable furs and a large bronze cauldron of steaming stew. We were each handed a flat black bowl and encouraged to eat our fill, washing it down with the same weak ale that we had all been drinking since we were weened from our mother's breasts.

The night in the branches of the Sacred Oak had not been a restful one, and so we were very happy to lie awhile on the soft mounds and relax, knowing that we were, at least for a while, safe from any pursuers.

Chapter 4

The Druids help

When we woke a few hours later it was to find a Druid standing over us. I asked him his name, only to be told that the Druids had no names, since they were as one.

Outside we found the others sitting on a circle of logs waiting patiently for us to share our story in more detail. We took the places left for us and waited.

"It would please us if you would tell us more of how you came to be on this road. And of the route you plan to follow with the torcs of your people".

I took a deep breath and began. They sat in respectful silence as I told them of my people's journey from the island in the west to the hill that we called the Caburn in the time of my grandfather's grandfather. Of our uneasy relationship with those who were already there when we arrived, of attack and counterattack. Loss after loss as blood feuds deepened, until a time had come when they had made the guardian on the slope across the vale and we had agreed some sort of peace with us keeping mainly to the high grounds, and they the low.

They were still as I told them of the day the Romans came, and how their Druid brethren were slaughtered during the rituals that they were bound to observe before any battle, and of how easily our warriors fell before the massed shields bristling with hardened tips of spear and sword.

When I spoke of the grey beast there was a stir, and when I told them how I saw my father and brother slain, and my mother and younger siblings tied and alone there were sighs of sympathy and sorrow. Finally, when I spoke again of the liberation of the torcs I could feel the intensity of their joined gaze, and then I was done.

"What you have said confirms all that we have already heard", said one of them from within the shade of a hood".

"We must prepare", said another.

"It is the time", said a third.

"What should we do?" I asked, looking around at the Elders of all the Druids, for these were surely they.

"There is much that must be done. You must go with your family here and take the torcs into the west for refuge".

“But I do not know the way”, I replied, feeling the emptiness of ignorance within me.

“One of us will go with you, for we also have sacred items that must be taken before the Romans and their allies come. These walls will hold strong against a Celt attack, bound as they are with spells and incantations, but there are new gods coming and their power is in the grey beast and the golden eagles, and against them our walls will not stand”.

Olwen spoke, for her a rare thing.

“What of the rest of you? Surely you cannot stay here”.

“We cannot. We must each go a separate way to the first line of beacons and light them when the night is darkest, and their light will travel furthest. That will set off the others and the land will know that there is danger coming. Then we will journey on and tell our brothers, and all of the peoples, of the Roman army that is marching north and west and of the grey beasts and the strong iron that they bring with them, and then the Chiefs of the north and west will have time to gather their forces and strengthen their strongholds as best they can. And those who chose to can take refuge in the Black Mountains beyond the great rivers, for that is the best that can be done ahead of the spreading evil of invasion".

There was nothing more that needed to be said and so we all left the meeting place and returned to our huts to prepare ourselves for our departure the next morning.

When I was lying in my bed, Olwen came over and knelt next to me. She took my hand in hers, bent over and whispered in my ear.

"Bran. The road ahead is a long one and my husband and I are old. I want you to promise me, that if we fall by the wayside you will not leave Galvyn and Alane. Promise me that you will take them with you".

Her grip was intense. I pushed myself up on my elbows.

"Nothing will happen to you". I replied.

"But if it does", she said, "if it does".

"I promise you, that I will stay with Galvyn and Alane and see them safe into the west", I said.

I knew that I would, and not for duty, but for love.

Chapter 5

The Forest surprises us

Our Druid came to the hut just before dawn. Olwen had already stoked the small fire and heated through the pottage. I lay where I had woken, with Galvyn tucked in beside me and watched him add some fresh green leaf, mushrooms and herbs to the mix. He was a young man. He moved with the grace of someone fit and strong, more hunter and warrior than Druid. He had a long moustache but no beard. His hair was tied back into a loose ponytail and above his brown eyes, there was one solitary woad mark on his forehead. On each thumb he wore a ring of heavy gold, with another on the middle finger of his left hand. He saw me looking at them and for the first time, I heard his mellifluous voice.

"These rings are made of Gold from the Western Mountains, the Lands of my Fathers. They are a mark of my family and of my position in that family before I took the path of the Oaken Druids. Each of us is permitted one such token of the lives that we came from. They speak in whispers to the gold still lying in the deep earth. They will help us find our way".

My shyness overcame me, my cheeks reddened, and I looked

down.

Olwen saved me and thanked him for the fresh produce of the woods. He nodded acceptance of her words and sat next to the fire. Even Druids felt the chill of the last of the night, it seemed. He spoke.

“We should wake them soon. This is a good day to travel and we have a great way to cover before we reach the crossing”.

“Is the going hard?” Asked Olwen.

“Not hard”, he replied, his voice kept low. The hills are gentle enough and the forests will prove welcoming when those who dwell there, man or spirit, see that you are with me and, maybe, sense the presence of the torcs.

“If they are so important?” The old women said, “how did they come to be in Bran’s hillfort. It is small and of little importance”.

Our Druid looked long into the flames lapping at the bottom of the blackened cauldron in which our breakfast was now bubbling.

“Alone, they are not. But all the torcs are made from gold from the same mine, far in the west. Their power grows as they get nearer to each other and to their home. We hope that our small mission will be one of many to take all the torcs back into the Black Mountains from whence they came, and that once they are all there, and safe, the energy that they draw from the Earth and the Sun and the Moon will be enough to protect this land and give us the strength to push the Romans back into the sea".

He paused staring, maybe thinking of the days ahead, with only an old man and me as the nearest things to warriors to protect our party.

"Wake them now".

Olwen reached across and put her hand with loving care on Macklyn's chest.

"Wake my love", she said, and I saw his eyes push open against the sticky glue of sleep and age. Then she rose and came to each of the others in turn to wake them with a touch, rather than words that might startle them too harshly from their dreams and so make them lose them. They took a moment to return, then sat up and stretched.

"Good morning to you all", said our new companion and friend,

“Eat well for this is the day that we must depart”.

Before I could eat, I felt the need to ease myself and walked off with Galvyn and Alane into the woods just outside the open gateway. We separated but stayed close enough to be safe, did what needed to be done, then returned to the comfort of our hut.

Having broken our fast and packed our few belongings into our bundles, we bade farewell to the gathered Druids at the gate and set off into the woods once more. This time I fell in with our guide and Macklyn took up the rear. I wanted to find out more about him and about the challenges that lay ahead.

“So, you were not you born a Druid in a Druid family?” was my first question. I know that there were female Druids and just wondered if they were a tribe of their own in some way.

“No”, he replied. “I was just an ordinary boy until my twelfth birthday. That was when the Druids of our village took me from the group of boys training outside the walls. They brought me to our Chief and my parents were asked to join us. My tunic was removed, and the Druids pointed out the mark on my thigh. A blue stain on my skin that they said marked me out as one who had been born to my parents but who had a different path to follow. It was then that they brought me to the Camp of the Great

Oak and began my training".

"How long ago was that".

"I am at the end of my twentieth summer now, so eight years have passed since I saw my family and my first home".

"Does that make you sad? It has only been a few full moons since I left my family behind, alive and dead, and my heart feels like a stone each morning when I wake".

"It is not for me to be happy or sad. It is what it is".

We walked in silence for a while. The conversation had brought my family vividly to mind and I did not want to lose the pictures.

It was evening before we thought of stopping again. The trees were thinning and the landscape more like heath than woodland. When we were still our guide stood with his head high and motionless. He almost seemed to be sniffing at the wind.

"There are red deer near", he said, "pointing into the east. "We should stay amongst the trees in case they startle. There may be wolves about. Both four legged and two".

We accepted his wisdom and settled in a clearing near another imposing Oak, which we could quickly climb if there was need. Alane, Galvyn and I went and gathered a little wood whilst Olwen foraged for mushrooms and berries. Alane and I were serious in our work, whilst Galvyn spent half his time in the trees and the other half on his knees, only pausing in between to jump on my back.

"Galvyn!" said Alane, "leave Bran alone! We need to gather food!"

The boy laughed and jumped up for a low branch to swing on. Alane smiled at me, and I took her smile and held it close.

We were eating when I felt the first slight vibration. Our eyes met and it was only a moment before we all reached the same decision and began to scramble up the tree. The Druid pushed us into the first branches before pulling himself up. It was only when I was already in the air that I noticed Macklyn and Olwen still on the ground, which was now trembling at the approach of the herd.

Too old to climb the tree with such speed, they had to take shelter in the lee of the trunk as the red deer burst, leaping and bucking into view. Forty or more, some of them young, but all with fear in their eyes.

We knew that the tree would protect us, since the deer meant none of us any harm. My worry though was why they were rushing through the woodland in such a tumult.

As they crashed past us, the answer became clear, for snapping at the heels of the herd were a pack of half a dozen long grey wolves, their heads low and snouts pushed out, with lolling tongues and razor teeth they pursued their terrified prey to the exclusion of all else, and that was our saving. They rushed past the tree without pause. Macklyn and I both had our boar spears at the ready and I would have sprung from the branch if the wolves had showed any sign of pause, but they did not and almost as soon as cavalcade had crashed upon us, it was gone.

After a few moments more we climbed down, our hearts settling. We touched each other for reassurance and then resumed our meal in silence. Done, we climbed the tree once more, this time all of us, so that we could sleep safely through the night, which passed without any further incident.

Chapter 6

Our party grows and illness strikes

The next day we left the trees and heathland behind us and after crossing a low area, we climbed the gentle slopes of the downs that mirrored our own. Here and there there were hillforts, some larger and many smaller than my own.

We decided that we would not invoke any of the customs of hospitality, unsure as we were of our welcome in these strange times, and so we made our way around them, trying to stay on high ground when we could, but ducking down into the woodland when there was a need to avoid contact.

Our Druid knew, from knowledge shared within, that the first of the truly great rivers ran twisting from west to east across the landscape, north of the hills in which we were currently travelling, and we headed not straight north but also to the west.

It was two days later that we struck one of the wide ways.

Normally these pathways were the routes taken by travelling smiths and other traders, and occasionally a war party when the occupants of one hillfort fell out with those of another, but on this day the way seemed busy with a ragtag collection of families and wanderers, most on foot but some with horses and even simple sledges or carts.

There was no threat that we could see from this straggling stream. We sat a while and watched them and could not make out any sort of command or leadership and so, since the wide way was by far the easiest going and the fastest route, we decided to join them.

No-one paid us any heed as we made our way diagonally down the final slope and found a place between two groups. After a little while being there felt natural and our group slowly merged with the one behind, where there was a boy of around my age.

Without plan or effort, we fell in step and walked side by side for some distance before we spoke to each other.

"My name is Bran", I began.

"I am Menw", he replied.

His accent was strange to me, but not so much that I could not understand him.

“We are travelling to the west”, I offered.

He smiled and said, “lucky for you then, that this road takes you that way”.

I realised the humour in what I had said and how he had answered it and smiled in return.

“I am travelling with my family”, said Menw. Then, in a quiet way. “We are fleeing the Romans”.

“Did they attack your home?” I asked.

“No”, he replied, “a Druid came to our hillfort. A Council was called. Our warriors tried to argue that we would fight the invaders. That this land was ours and that they should not push us off it. But the Elders took a different view. They favoured life in a different land over death and slavery in the land they once owned”.

“They made the right choice”, I said. “My fort was not warned. One day the Romans just came. Our Druids taunted them and died. Our warriors charged them and died. We tried to defend our gates against a great grey armoured beast, and more died. Now my father and brother are dead. My mother and the others are enslaved, at best. And I am seeking refuge in the west with these, my new family".

He looked at me curiously, "why is there a Druid in your party. Surely he cannot be part of your family".

Even though I instinctively liked Menw, I did not know him well enough to trust him with the secret of the three torcs and so I did not answer, since lying was against our code. He understood from my silence that I could not tell him rather than would not tell him, and so he let it pass.

"What is your plan when you get to the west?" I asked.

He smiled again. "We have no plan, other than to stay ahead of the Romans until such a time as they stop coming forward across the land".

"Why should they stop?" I asked, "I do not see that any of our peoples can stop them. Even the sea cannot stop them for they crossed that to get to us".

"We will soon be in the country of the Atrebates", Menw replied, "They are more fearsome than any of the other tribes and their warrior clans are bigger", it may be that they will stop the

Romans".

"Or it may be", said Mackyn who had fallen in alongside us without us realising, "that the Romans will decide that they have taken enough land and enough slaves and hunting dogs and grain and gold and set up a border and build within it".

"Or they may just go". This from our Druid who was also now with us. "In the stories from the Elders, they tell of an invasion such as this in the time of their grandfathers, and in that time the Romans came and took what they wanted and went away again".

There was silence for a while.

"But perhaps", I said, "their storytellers have retold the tales of that time to their new leaders, and those stories have fuelled their greed and that is why they are back, and that is why they might stay".

The Sun moved across the sky and the Moon came and went a few more times without incident, and then it was that day.

There was no warning that a terror was about to strike Macklyn down.

In the mid-day he was walking in front of Menw, Alane, Galvyn and me, as he had done for many days, using the boar spear as a staff to aid him and with Olwen close by.

At first, I thought that he had just stumbled over a stone or pothole in the path, but he did not recover his balance and fell to one knee with only the staff stopping him from falling to the ground. Olwen gave a sharp little cry and bent down to hold his shoulders, but she was not strong enough and he toppled to his left and crumpled into the dust, pulling her down with him.

We all ran and gathered around him as Olwen gathered herself and pulled his cloak away from his mouth and slid a knee beneath his head to support him.

His face was strange. His left eye seemed to have been dragged down his face as if by an invisible claw, which had continued to pull down his cheek and mouth. He was dribbling and making noises in which, somewhere, there were words. His left arm and leg were twitching and jerking, and a stain spread across his groin and left thigh for he had wet himself.

People stopped and looked but there was no-one who could offer help until our guide came back to us, having gone someway ahead to talk to others and see if he could learn more about the journey in front of us. He put his hand on the old man's chest, looked long into his eyes, then spoke his wisdom to us.

"I have seen this before in the Elders. There never seems to be a reason, but it is always one half of the body only. I know of a tree, the bark of which when boiled in water until it is dark then drunk, can aid in their recovery. Stay close here, the tree grows often over the banks of rivers where they are said to weep into the stream, and the first of the great rivers runs not far to our north. Try to keep him calm and I will be back as quickly as I can".

And with those words he was gone.

Even though the trickle of people was only that and not a great flow, we decided to move Macklyn into the shade of a tree by the wide ways edge. It took all of us to move him, especially since the task was made more difficult by his writhing and twisting in our grip. After a long while, with Olwen stroking his hair, he calmed down and seemed to drift off into a dreamy condition, part of this world, part of the next. The rest of us just sat, not feeling like talking. Alane and Galvyn were crying quietly to themselves and I went and sat with them and put my arms around them. In this way we waited patiently for the Druid to return with the medicine from the weeping tree.

It came to my mind that Menw had been with us when Macklyn was struck down. Startled by the thought I straightened and looked around. He was there, with his mother and father, only a few steps away. When his father saw me looking, he stood and came to me.

"I know that we have not known each other for more than a few days, but Menw has become your friend and he has asked that we stay and help you if we can, so we will await the Druid's return and if there is a way that Macklyn can go on, we will be a part of that, and if he does not recover, we will be here for that also".

I thanked him, and smiled across at Menw, hoping and praying that they would be helping us to continue on our way.

The day was almost done when the Druid returned. He had a bag full of bark which he told me he had cut from three different willow trees for luck. One square from each, a hands width across, so as not to hurt the trees.

He took the bark out and used a sharp flint to scrape the pink flesh from the underside. Whilst he did that, Alane and Menw's mother prepared a small fire and a tripod of branches on which to hang the Druids small iron pot. They added water and began to heat it. He cut the pink shreds into ever smaller pieces and added them, stirring as he went and intoning under his breath words that I could only partly make out and knew that I was forbidden to speak. Time passed and his face told us that he was not content. He stood and looked around thinking, then he called me over. He pulled me close and raised his cloak to shield us.

"We must place the torcs in the brew", he said", we will need their power to help Macklyn to recover but keep them shielded. We do not want to tempt anyone on the way into a bad deed".

So hidden I reached into my tunic where the torcs were concealed around my stomach and took them out. Unwrapping each, kissing it and asking for permission, he placed them in the pot, then continued with his low chanting till the water had gone down by half. At that point he put the small cauldron to one side and covered it with a cloth embroidered with runic signs to allow it to cool.

We were all sitting around Macklyn, each with one hand upon him. We felt that this contact would calm and reassure him, and he was, after a while quieter. Olwen was whispering into his ear, but I could not hear what she said.

When the liquid was cool enough The Druid brought it over, still covered by the cloth. He asked us to turn away, even me although I knew the secret contents of the pot, and so I could only listen as he lifted Macklyn's head and gently poured the brew, sip by soothing sip, into his twisted mouth.

When it was all gone, Olwen turned and took his head again and cradled it in her lap and we all replaced our hands. The Druid had turned away and carefully and respectfully wrapped the torcs in their cloth. That done he returned them to me and I retied them around my stomach where they would sit invisibly beneath my loose woollen tunic.

We stayed grouped around the old man all through that long, slow night, lying where we could keep our touch on him, reassured by the warmth that came from him and the pulse of blood below his skin.

When the sun finally began to lighten the eastern sky the world around us began to stir. Up and down the wide way in both directions the little communities that had set up their camps began to pack up their bedding and their pots and prepare for the next few thousand steps of their long journey away from the threat of the Romans and into the west.

I looked anxiously at Macklyn. His eyes were closed, and he was still, in Olwen's all-embracing arms. The Druid was kneeling next to him with his hand upon the old man's chest, which I now saw was rising and falling slowly in the pale dawn.

"We should stay and rest", I said. "I don't think that Macklyn will be able to travel for a moon's coming and passing at least".

After a moment the Druid turned his face to me. I could see a great sadness in his eyes.

"We cannot", he replied. "If we stay here more than seven days, maybe less, the Romans may well come upon us. And if not the Romans there will be brigands along this way waiting for a gap in the stream or a solitary traveller to pray on. It is too dangerous for us to stop".

"But what else can we do?" I could feel tears in my chest because I knew what he would say".

"We must do the right thing for us all, for Macklyn too".

"What is that?" I asked, knowing full well what the answer would be. The Code was clear. The Elders should be nurtured and cared for when it was possible to do so, but when the burden of their age became too great for the community to deal with, they should be sent peacefully on their way to meet the Gods, with all due ceremony and respect".

"If you had all stayed at their farm in the woods, and he had become ill in this way. He could have been fed and kept clean and maybe, after a season or two, he would have recovered enough, but that was not a decision that you could make".

"I know we could not", I said, "Because the Romans were coming and staying would have meant slavery or death for all of us".

"I know", the Druid said quietly, "there is no blame in this, unless you blame age and the invaders. It is their conspiracy that has led us here".

All through this exchange Olwen had been sitting, with her head down, looking at Macklyn's quiet face and listening to us. Alane was next to me, and I put my arm around her in a way that I hoped was comforting. She turned her face briefly to me, half smiled in a sad way and turned back, but my arm was accepted.

"I will not leave him now", Olwen said, "We have been together since our fourteenth summer. We made a daughter and she made these children with us here. He and I built a house and a farm together. He nursed me when I was ill, and I him. I will not leave him now. You do not need to help him on his way. I am his wife, and I will help him stay".

Olwen's love for her husband had power and the Druid, in response, touched his heart in respect.

"But there is one thing that I must ask of you", she continued. "I ask you to take Galvyn and Alane with you into the west".

Both of the children reacted instantly, leaping up and wrapping their arms around the woman who had brought them up as a mother. Both were crying and both were saying, over and over again, "no, no, no, we will not go".

Olwen held them both tight, kissing them on the hair and face many times, crying quietly and whispering into their ears that they must. That there was a time when it was right for the old to pass into memory and that this was that time for her and for Macklyn, stricken as he was.

I cried also, sitting nearby, hoping beyond hope that something else would happen and change the path that seemed to lay before us.

The Druid, taking in the love of the family for each other looked at me to include me and then held out a desperate hope.

"I have seen this before. This sudden attack without warning or reason. I have seen people regain their strength, and I have seen others almost frozen who would die if not fed and cared for. I have given Macklyn the first bark and we should give that time to work".

"But we cannot stay here", I said, "you have already said that if we do, we face slavery or death".

"When faced with two impossible answers, the wise step back and look for a third way. We must give Macklyn time, but we cannot stay here, so we must find a way of moving him to a safer place".

Olwen was looking at him now, as were the children, their eyes wide, their cheeks wet with tears.

"Is there a way?" Olwen asked, with fear and hope in her voice.

"There may be", the Druid replied", Bran, make some more of the bark brew, you know the way now. I will return before the darkness falls".

And with that he was gone. I made the brew as before, being careful to shield the torcs from prying eyes. When it was ready Olwen fed it to Macklyn, using the edge of her robe to place it, drop by precious healing drop, between his wracked lips.

In this way the day passed, as we waited anxiously for the Druid's return. It was Galvyn who saw him first. Springing up he pointed down the way.

"Look, look, he is coming. It's him, I'm sure it's him", which it was.

The Druid was walking alongside a large man leading a horse, behind which a wooden cart bumped along. It's four large wheels seeming to twist in the furrows of the well-travelled way.

By the time they reached us Galvyn, Alane and I were on our feet, excited by the unusual sight and realising that here was the means by which Macklyn could be moved to a place of safety.

"You have done it!" I exclaimed. "Where did you find such a thing?"

"Where there are people on the move", said our friend and guide", there will always be people willing to help them on their way".

The man snorted, "for a price, yes!"

"Always for a price", the Druid replied, looking sideways at him, "so it is fortunate that I had the price upon me and was able to pay. He will take us to the crossing, a month away".

It was then I noticed that the two thumb rings were gone, and that the third, which had been on his middle finger, was now on the first finger of his right hand. The realisation of what he had done made me take my breath in sharply. He noticed this, as he seemed to notice all things, and smiled a most gentle smile, but for now, said nothing.

The man looked back at him. "So long as the Atrebates let us pass. If they do not. There is no other way, and you may have to give up the third of those pretty rings of yours to open the gates to their lands.

The cart was already well loaded with goods, for the man was a trader who made his living selling pots and knives and flints to the villages and forts along the road. Even though he had been well paid, he was not willing to lose any of his stock. Some bags were placed across the broad back of his horse, and the others were given to the rest of us to carry. The Druid had by far the largest sack, but even so it seemed light to him.

We lifted Macklyn into the flat space that had been cleared, after lining it first with our cloaks, and when he was comfortable, we set off.

The going was steady, as the wide way threaded its way along the lower slopes of the gently rising hills. Low enough to be easy going but high enough to be clear of any boggy ground or areas of forest that might slow our progress.

In this way twenty-seven days and more slipped by. Each evening we made a simple camp and the Druid, and I made more of the barks brew for Olwen to feed to Macklyn. We ourselves lived on the vegetable stew made from whatever we could find, having to turn down offers of meat from hunters who made their way up and down the road offering their catch to whoever had the means to pay for it.

It was around mid-day, with the sun as high as it was going to reach in the falling of the year when we reached the edge of the lands of the Atrebates. Before us was a broad valley and beyond that ridges of low hills that seemed to almost drift in the blue mists.

Directly below us was a sight such as I had never seen.

A huge collection of shelters thrown up with no thought or plan. Campfires burned, sending thin trails of smoke into the leaden sky. There were people everywhere, more people than I imagined could exist. Children ran around in groups, with dogs barking playfully at their heels.

"We are here", the Cartman said. "We have reached the border of the Atrebates".

He led us down the final stretch of road and into the sprawling mass. Even though no path had been visible from the outside, we did find ourselves on a well-defined way that twisted and turned between the jumble of huts and shelters. These became more substantial as we got deeper into the camp and I assumed that this was the case because the people in the centre had been there the longest.

I heard many accents in the voices around me, but mostly the same language, the language of the southern peoples. The people who were running in front of the advancing Romans, or whose settlements had already been destroyed.

As we went in ever deeper the huts and twisting paths began to have a sense of permanence. There were many pits, some capped with clay but most still open, evidence that there had been at least some farming, or else they would have had nothing to store.

Our Carter eventually brought us out in an open space which I imagined was somewhere near the centre of the new village. I was not surprised by the conversation between him and a tall man who had come from somewhere to bar our way. He showed interest in where we had come from only in as far as it updated his knowledge of the Roman advance, but he showed more interest in our plans for the immediate future. The Druid intervened:

"We are travelling into the west. There we have business with the Hillmen and my Brother Druids. We will though need to rest before we pass on".

A sad smile accompanied by a dropping of the eyes and a soft exhalation through his nose told me, even before he spoke, that his words would not be those that I wished to hear.

"Friends", he began, "I myself arrived here when there were no huts, only a few dozen tents thrown quickly up against the rain that drives up this wide valley, and that was only two moons ago. I too wanted to make my way into the west, to take my family to safety, but I found that I could not".

"Why not?" asked our Druid, "This road is well trodden and has been taken by many in both directions since before stories have been told. What holds you back now?"

"This camp marks the edge of the lands of the Atrebates. They have now decided that the way will be closed to all but the wealthy".

"But why", I asked", do not the customs mean that free passage must be given to all".

The tall man looked down at me. "Yes, in most times, but these are not those. There are many in the tribe who fear that the tide of refugees will wash up on the low hills in the west and be pushed back and that they, we, will stay in their lands since the Romans seem intent on taking control of ours. They think that our needs will conflict with theirs and that the best thing that they can do is to stop us entering their lands at all".

With that, he turned away and we understood that we should follow him to the place where we could settle.

Chapter 7

The Camp

I did not realise, as we made our way from that central space through the teeming mass of refugees, just how long we would remain in that camp.

No-one paid us much attention as we passed the first few huts in this western part of the settlement, if huts are how they should be named for they were not built like any that I had seen before.

These were tall and pointed, some as high as four tall men and just as wide. From what I could see they were made of long poles wrapped in various cloths and skins stitched roughly together into a patchwork covering, with a smoke hole at the top.

There was no real path here, just a slightly wider series of gaps just wide enough for the cart, that led us naturally towards the newest area, but that was still a long way off. Here also there were craftsman working, toiling to make the pots and tools that the ever-growing population would need.

Eventually we came to another open space and the tall man showed us where we could pile up our meagre belongings.

“The woods on that low slope will provide you with poles long enough to make your shelter”, he said, “the coverings you must make or barter for, for there are none spare”.

“I have never seen shelters like these”, I said, inviting an explanation by the tone of my voice.

“Nor had any of us”, he answered.” When the first arrived and realised that they would be here a long while, they tried to build round huts, but there is no wattle, and the thatch belongs to the Atrebates. When they realised this, they experimented with lean-to’s and long tents and then, one day, one of them came up with the structure you now see all around you. It was clearly the simplest and the quickest way to protect themselves from the wind and the rain and if the covering at the base is thick hide properly weighted, from animals too”.

After pointing out a few more things, the way to the nearest safe water upstream, the area where we should go to relieve ourselves downstream.

Menw, Galvyn and I took on to ourselves the task of gathering wood for the night’s fire whilst Alane went for water and Olwen made Macklyn as comfortable as she could. The Carter began to rearrange the cart as soon as Macklyn was taken from it.

“I have work to do here”, he said. “These people will buy my goods from me, and at a good price. When I have done my trading, I will be back to see if you have found an answer to the blockade. If you have, I will help you onwards. If you have not, then my job is done, and I will head back to refill my wagon before I return in the spring”, and with that he turned his cart around and disappeared into the throng that seemed to ebb and flow around us.

The next morning, as we ate our small morning meal, we talked of our position. Olwen spoke first, since Macklyn could not, although his eyes had become clearer in the days since the Druid had begun to treat him with the willow bark.

“We must find a way to cross the lands of the Atrebates. It is in the west that we will find safety, and we must have a peaceful place to live if we are to make my husband well”.

There was a long silence. We all stared at the ground, mostly overwhelmed by the problems that beset us. In front the warriors of the Atrebates were an ever-present obstacle, around us an ever-increasing mass of refugees competed for the sparse resources, and somewhere behind us the Romans were advancing with seemingly unstoppable force. It was the Druid who spoke.

"The Atrebates are of this land, as are we. There will be Druids in their lands, as there are in the lands of all the peoples. They will soon realise, if the war leaders do not, that this flow of people will not cease and that, at some point, the dam of sorrow that they have built with their fear will break and the tide will sweep towards the west. When they see that future, they will choose another and let us pass".

But I had a thought that worried me.

"But might it not be true that the Atrebates see us as a first line of defence against the Roman's grey beasts? At least a way of giving them time to further prepare".

Another silence, and then a deep breath.

"They will have heard by now of the fate of Maiden Hill. The largest hillfort in the land. Defended by thousands of warriors behind mighty ramparts. Destroyed in less time than it takes to dig a pit and most of those inside killed. There is no defence in these open lands. We must go or we must die, or else live our lives as slaves of the Romans".

Olwen raised her eyes to his. In them were all the sorrows of the common people. I felt Alane's hand slip into mine, and I held it firmly, trying not to transmit my fear to her.

Olwen spoke and her words were those of a woman with a family she loved and wanted to protect. “There is another way… We could just accept their rule. Treat for peace with them and give them tribute from our crops, as we have for centuries to the warrior kings of one tribe or another. Since our food will be taken anyway, does it matter much to us who is taking it?”

The Druid replied. “The Romans are different. Our masters at least speak our tongue and worship our Gods and know our ways. The Romans will take whatever they want, whenever they want, to wherever they want. To them, we are beasts of burden, nothing more, and that is why we must go”.

We all knew that the Druid’s words had the power of truth and our path became clear, but the summer was ending and we all also knew that within the span of the next moon the rains would sweep in from the great sea and the rivers would fill till their banks were breached and the waters would flow out across the meadows until the plains before us were a great sluggish lake across which only skilled boatmen could cross, and then only if they dared between the squalls and storms that would turn the winding currents into deadly traps.

No-one travelled far after the sun had sunk so low that even at mid-day our shadows were long. The view of all we spoke to was that the Romans would hold fast until the spring and that we, therefore could do the same. If we were wrong, we would see the beacons to the south and east lit far before the Romans could reach us, and so we should settle and build against the storms and wait for the waters to fall. This would also give time for Macklyn to heal, and so that was what we decided to do.

The question now arose of a dwelling fit for that purpose. We decided to follow the example of those who would now be our neighbours. The woods did prove to be a plentiful source of the long poles that we needed and soon we had the eight that our new home would be made of. Menw and I went hunting also and came back with a small deer, parts of which we were able to barter for some hemp twine. Then came the matter of construction.

Each pole was the length of three men and needed to be tied together where they crossed, far beyond our reach. We sat looking at them a while, each trying different ways inside our heads. Menw shared his idea first.

"We can lay the posts on the ground, crossing where they will need to cross when up, and tie them tight there. One of us can then hold up the centre whilst three others brace the poles and move them in a handspan at a time. As the centre rises, the knots should tighten".

"And, if we sharpen the posts where they touch the ground", I added, "the weight of the poles will push them in and make the whole thing stronger".

"Then", offered Alane, "we can rest the other poles against those three and wrap the long end of the twine round them. Looping it over at the last and tying it at head height!"

This was clearly a good method and so we began. The poles were sturdy so some men from near-by lent us a hand to steady them as they rose above us. The tripod worked well, and resting the extra poles, spaced out, around them was easy enough, but getting the twine tight against the apex proved hard. It kept snagging and would not sit well. One of our neighbours briefly left, returning with a long thin pole with a fork in the end. With this he guided the twine into the narrow spaces, lifting and looping it over each pole in turn, and soon the job was done.

We lacked the number of hides and blankets needed to make a full cover, so we made as large a half-circle shape as we could and wrapped it around the lower part, saving enough to provide a flat cover for the narrowing opening. When we had done, the same neighbour bunched the cloth at the flat centre and tied a twine to it, which he then guided over the apex with his forked stick. When he pulled the twine, the centre rose to make a low cone, from which, as we were soon to discover, the rain would flow off to the side of our new home.

Chapter 8

Making do

We did not then know how long we would be in that tent in that ever-growing camp on the low slopes above the wide plain. We did know that we would have to fend for ourselves in most respects. None here had much spare to give us, nor would we have expected them to.

Now that we had a home of sorts, the daily challenge was to keep ourselves fed. We saw little of the Druid in those days and Macklyn, although better, was still not well enough to do anything for himself let alone for the rest of us, so it fell to me, Menw and Galvyn to hunt and fish whilst Olwen and Alane would forage and keep the camp.

The problem was that we were few amongst many, and all of the many had the same needs as we few. Those who had been here for a while had already stripped the nearby wild lands of fruits and nuts and so it was mainly fungus and mushrooms that the women brought home.

In the same way, smaller animals had been hunted to extinction in the forest for a day's hunting in all directions and the deer and the pigs had already learned to stay well away.

The stretch of riverbank that our Atrebates captors gave us access to was crowded during the day and Menw and I were no fisherman. It was though good for us that Galvyn had lived most of his life with Olwen and Macklyn on the banks of a small river and so he knew what he was doing, and after the first catch-less day, he tried to lead us upstream to waters that were less disturbed, only to find that we were turned back by the mounted horsemen who had been tasked with keeping us here.

His answer was to make a small coracle which he could paddle out into the lazy stream. He was skilled in the handling of this flimsy craft and so he was able to succeed where others could not. At first the Atrebates rode up the bank at speed, thinking that he was trying to cross but when they realised that he was only fishing, they let him be. His other trick was to fish at night, when the light of a flaring torch would bring the fish to him as if drawn by his need to his hand.

Galvyn was proud that it was he, the youngest of us, who was the most successful at getting us food. So successful was he in fact, that we were able to trade the fish that we did not need for things that we did.

The first trades were to get us more hides and cloths so that we could raise the roof of our tent higher, even to the point where the beams crossed. There, using a tying pole, we were able to fashion an opening and thereafter we could keep a small fire lit inside the tent, which was a comfort to Macklyn in the dark hours.

Once news of our growing community spread across the surrounding hills professional tradesman and makers started coming to the camp, bringing with them the flat black dishes that we used so much and tools of flint and bronze as well as those of iron, although those were worth more than any number of fish that we could catch.

None-the-less, as time passed our lives settled into yet another routine of daily hunting, fishing and foraging. The wave of refugees slowed to steady series of ripples and from this we worked out that the Romans had stopped their advance in preparation for the coming rains and sleets of the winter months when the rivers would swell, and the pathways become nothing more than endless sucking swamps of mud and filth.

Macklyn was strengthening with the passing days until on one grey dawn, he spoke words that we could understand for the first time since he had been struck down. Those words were, "Thank you", and he spoke then to Olwen as she held his hand in love.

It was also at this time that Galwyn got himself into trouble with the Council. This group of Elders had assumed the natural authority of their age and made decisions on behalf of us all on matters that concerned the camp as a whole.

One of the rules that had been agreed early on was that there would be no fighting. Galwyn was not a boy given to brawling, even in play, and it was so a great surprise to us when we were called before one of the Council. Galwyn was kneeling in front of them, his head down and his tunic torn, along with three other boys of about the same age.

"Stand forth those of you who are responsible for these rule-breakers".

The Councillor's tone was sombre. I stood forward along with three others, as was the way. Had Macklyn been able it would have been him, for in matters such as this the men took precedence first by blood and then by age. We did not speak but stood behind the boy for whom we had been called out.

"These boys by the river this morning, broke the way by fighting within the camp. This as you all know is forbidden. The fact of this is not in dispute. Now, before punishment is decided you have been called to listen to their pleas. Each case must be heard, and each of you will be responsible for carrying out my judgment. This is the way."

The other three boys stood as one. Heads bowed they exchanged glances then one of them, the largest of the three, spoke.

"We were on the riverbank trying for fish. We do this every day. You all know that. We had been there since before first light, doing our best, but we had caught nothing, not even by using our torchlights. Then he came by. Five fish he had. Big fish from the deep waters, caught from that little boat thing that he uses, and we asked him for a fish, just one, one of the five, and he laughed at us and turned up his lip and said "no" and this made us angry".

The Councillor waited then spoke. "And so, you went for him, in your rage?"

"We did". The boy replied. "I know ... we know that it was wrong to do so but we were hungry and our families were hungry and we knew that we had failed them and when he sneered like that it was as if the sounds of the day were dimmed and the edges of my sight glowed red and before I even knew, I was on him and the others too and he was on the ground but we didn't stop, and I am sorry for that".

As the boy told his tale I stared at the back of Galvyn's neck and I saw there a different red from the haze of anger his attacker had described. I saw a red born of shame. Shame that he had broken the code of hospitality that was so important to us all.

The Councillor turned his attention to Galvyn, whose gaze was fixed firmly on the ground.

"Is that the way of it?" he asked.

Galvyn took a moment to respond, but then he raised his head and looked at the Councillor straight and in a bare whisper just said,

"Yes … Yes, and I am sorry for it".

The Elder looked about the enclosing circle, picking out those men who had come here to be responsible for these boys.

"They are not yet of their twelfth year? Am I right in that?"

I nodded with the others.

"This then is my judgment. Those three who did the beating must be beaten. Those men here who are responsible must carry out that punishment. But when you do show care. The boy Galvyn is bruised but uncut and so the boys who attacked him must be bruised but uncut. As to Galvyn, he had fish to give and did not give it, and in the not giving he belittled these others so provoking their anger. It is my judgement that he must help provide the others with a coracle each and train them in its use and in the ways of a fisherman and on each day until that training is complete, he must give each of them a fish, so long as fish are caught. The first three each day".

The assembled people nodded in agreement, as did I. It was a wise judgment. The three attackers would learn to curb their anger. Galvyn would learn humility. More families would be fed, and more boys trained in how to feed them, whilst we would go without the extras that those fish could have been traded for which, since Galvyn was a youth in our family, was fair.

The next day the boys arrived at our shelter and I took them, with Galvyn, down the rivers bank and into the woods to find the willow tree that we would need. We each carried a sharp blade and so we were able to make short work cutting and stripping enough thin branches to build the frame of the coracles. When we were done Galvyn turned to me.

"Can you let me speak with these others as if you were not here?"

He knew that this far from the camp I would not leave them, even if he had asked me to. I nodded and said nothing. Galvyn stood and faced the other three.

“I was wrong. I should have given you some fish and I should not have looked at you as I did. You were beaten for your response to what I did, and I don’t think we can be friends until that is sorted”.

At that he stopped talking and pulled his tunic over his head. He let it drop and picked up three of the willow wands, handing one to each of the other boys.

“I want you to beat me as you were beaten. Then I will teach you what I know, and we can be friends”.

He turned his bare back to them and braced himself against the nearby trunk. The falling branches of the willow enclosed the scene. The boys looked at each other and then at me. I kept my face blank and did not move. One by one they raised up the sticks and moved to form a semi-circle around Galvyn. I saw his shoulders tense as he sensed their position. As one they raised their arms, as one they brought them whistling down and, as one, they stopped a fingers width short before pressing the sticks gently on to his naked skin. Then they laughed and threw them down. Kicked his legs out from beneath him and ended up in a giggling pile. When they had calmed down enough to speak the dark one spoke up.

"We deserved what we got, and it was nothing new to us! Your offer was enough. Teach us what you know, and we will fish together".

And with that they collapsed into a tangled heap again.

When their game was done, we carried on with the serious business of making the coracles. The thin willows, freshly cut, were ideal for the task and soon each of the boys had created a basket big enough for them to sit in. I had brought enough hide with me, given to me by their families since it was precious. These we attached to one rim with sinew and gut string having made holes with sharp bone needles. Then each helped the others to pull the hide tight across the shape of the vessels until it became clear where the holes should be punched to secure the second edge. Each boy could then carefully fold and shape the skins, stitching as they went until the shallow bowls were complete.

One paddle for each boy had been roughly hewn by an Uncle of the dark-haired boy, whose name we now knew to be Sloan, with enough wood left to allow for finishing and personal carvings so that each became a personal thing.

The boys chatted as they worked, telling the stories of how they came to be here, and the stories were much the same. Of the Roman army marching into their forts and villages. Of fire and fear and fleeing, or of local tribes with a history of trade and contact using the arrival of the Romans to settle old debts and jealousies. But all the stories ended the same way, with long arduous journeys across emptying landscapes as the people fled into the west.

By the time they were all done the sun was low on the hills and we made our way back to the camp in good time for the evening meal. They parted as friends and Galvyn came back with me to our hearth.

"That was a brave thing you did", I said", they could have given you a hard beating, three on one as they were".

He looked up at me with that crocked smile of his and answered me.

"And if they had I would have taken it and we would still have become friends".

Now it was my turn to smile down at him. I threw an arm around his shoulder and pulled him close as we walked the final paces realising that young in years though he was, he was even so becoming a man.

In the weeks that followed we saw little of Galvyn. He was up and out early returning only as the sun set. Each day he would meet his friends and they would, with increasing skill and success, go out onto the river and catch fish, often enough to feed their families and more. The extra, they traded in the small market that had developed at the centre of the camp. There were few coins about so each transaction was a long debate around how many fish were worth so many of something else.

In the afternoons they would take to the woods close to the camp where, I later discovered, they were building an increasingly large camp of their own having secured a small axe and many lengths of twine. Other boys had joined them now and Galvyn soon began to sleep there too, coming to see us only to give us our generous share of his catch.

And so, the time passed as the winter set in. The rains had now become the weather that we expected every day and the river began to swell and deepen and spread. Our bank was the higher of the two and I was standing on it when the other failed and the waters surged out across the plain. We had already stopped the boys fishing until this happened and the waters settled into their new course. What had been the river now became a great lake the far shore of which was barely visible. The water was leaden and grey reflecting the heavy sky above it, and safe enough after a few days for the boys to fish again.

Of the Atrebates there was no sign. I suppose they now assumed that the water was too wide for us to cross which, here at least, it was.

Chapter 9

News from the West

The days had become as one, except that each was shorter than the one before and so I cannot tell how many had passed when our Druid returned. We were sitting around our hearth wreathed in dark smoke, inside now that the weather was so poor, when he was suddenly just there sitting beside me and reaching his bowl out to the cauldron of steaming greens and fish. We all ate in silence. When the meal was done, we wiped the bowls clean with course bread, drank a mouthful of ale, and waited in expectation. He looked around and spoke.

"I have been to the West and spoken with my brothers there. They brought me to the fort of the Prince who rules in the Celtic hills. I told him of this camp and the hundreds who now languish here, their way barred. He knew something of it already and was well briefed about the doings of the Romans. His word is that you are all welcome. He said to me that when the Romans wash up on the shores of his lands the more people who are there to block their way the better the outcome might be".

I asked the question that everyone had in their heads.

"But what of the Atrebates and their chariots? They have said that we can not enter their lands and to go any other way would take us too far east and north, and in the east, we might find Romans and, in the north, the wild tribes?"

"On my journey back, I stopped at the high fort at the heart of the Atrebates tribal land. As a Druid they gave me shelter and, for that and other reasons, access to their Elders. I explained to them that passage was guaranteed and that they would not find this camp simply moved from the outside of this border to the inside of the next. When that was clear to them, they gave permission for everyone here to make the journey".

The news made as all happy and we were anxious to spread it. Soon there was a gathering in the centre of the camp where people spoke excitedly of the Druids report, hoping that it was true but needing to hear it from his own lips.

When our Druid appeared, the chattering fell away. He relayed the news that he had told us in tones of calm authority. When he had finished the Elders, in a tight huddle, discussed together what their recommendations should be. Eventually the oldest of them stood to address us all.

"Given the news from the Prince of the High hills. We feel that we should all prepare to leave. That we should travel together into the west and that when we are there, having received the welcome of the Prince and his people, we will ask for a remote hill and become a settlement that will thrive in their protection, in the safety of the Black Mountains".

There were murmurs of agreement from all around. Galvyn and his friends were dancing around each other, happy that they would now not be separated when the camp broke up.

Planning began. The shelters would break down into long sledges, which could be used by those who had no carts. The frozen months ahead would make it easier to drag these across the ground, even by those who had no horses or oxen to take the strain.

But behind all the excitement and joy was the dark shadow of the Romans behind us and the great flood in front.

The most seasoned amongst us at dealing with rivers watched the swirling, debris-filled waters daily, waiting for a sign that the rains had stopped in the mountains to the north-west and that a passage further upstream, would therefore be possible.

One fine day they decided that they could see a lessening in the flow and a slight drop in the levels and the order was given to move. Our little family packed the last few items and prepared to leave the village that had become our home for many moons. Macklyn was able to walk now, with the aid of Olwen and a thick staff, at least well enough to keep up with the slow pace of the caravan of refugees which was good news indeed, for of the Carter and his cart, we had heard no more.

We headed east and north, the thinking being that as we moved upstream the banks would close and we would find a place to cross and after four long, slow days, we found a bend where the river had narrowed enough that a tall fallen tree could bridge it. The order was given, and a band of warriors armed with sharp axes, were sent to explore the nearby wooded land.

Were it not for the horses and livestock, we could have made a bridge from twine and flat boards, but we were too burdened for that. The men returned before night fell with four straight trunks that were long enough. These were then split with the wedges carried by some for just that purpose and eight flat lengths were soon ready. A group with strong horses rode then swam then rode across the deep narrows taking with them long ropes, that were already tied into notches on the end of the bridging timbers. The first of the split trunks were then rolled to the edge of the bank, side on, and twisted so that almost half its length was already across the gap before anyone needed to pull. Boys sat on the end furthest from the bank as the plank was dragged forward on the small rollers that had been pushed beneath it. These were swiftly pulled back as they made the edge, ready for re-use with the next piece. In this way all eight sections were pulled forward and a broad crossing was created.

At a given signal the rest of us began to cross in twos and threes. Finally, the oxen and the horses were taken over one at a time and soon we all stood on the far bank.

There was a discussion then about whether to leave the bridge in place or to pull the far side clear and let it be swept away by the strong currents below. Some argued that we should but, in the end, it was decided to leave it for any small group of travellers who might need to cross who would not be able to build a bridge of their own. The Romans, it was thought, would have no problem building a bridge of their own strong enough to carry their mass, so destroying ours would at most, gain us a half a day.

For the first few days the Atrebates riders flanked us, appearing occasionally against the bleak skyline as they crossed the ridges that edged the wide valley through which we travelled. Since we had the permission of their Chieftain to cross, we were not harassed by any of the villages or forts that we passed, and we soon left the wide expanse of that first great river behind us.

The Druid had done his work well and so he was able to guide us into the west by a northerly route, only bringing us to the next great river where there was a chance of crossing it.

Our journey now took us through a soft landscape of gentle hills and escarpments. Each evening we stopped to make a temporary camp with the last of us arriving an hour after the first. We were fortunate that it was our friend who led the way and so we had the first choice of camp site and a little longer to rest. Once or twice the local people would bring us a carcass of a slaughtered pig or come to show us where a deer might be found and we would eat well, but most times it was whatever greens we could find.

It was on an evening such as this that Alane and I began to sit together at the hearth, a move much welcomed by Macklyn and Olwen, who I had come to think of as my mother and father in the months since the attack on the Caburn. Even so, my dreams were still haunted by the image of my father and brother lying twisted on the field of battle and by the imagined experiences of my mother and my siblings since they had fallen into the hands of the Romans.

It was during one such night terror that Alane came and pushed her little brother away and came to hold me in her arms until the shaking stopped and my tears dried on my cheeks. After that she stayed.

After many days of slow travel, we reached the last brow before the next natural obstacle to our progress. The great river that this time flowed from north to south and which twisted like a great snake before us. It was another cause for worry but also for hope, for beyond it we could see the hills rising that would become the Black Mountains, our final refuge from our advancing Roman enemies.

A day later we were on the rivers bank. Although we had travelled north as well as west the water was still wide and deep and there was no safe way that we could cross it without help. As always, someone had taken the opportunity to set up a little enterprise and there were any number of sturdy river craft moored below us, each of which would carry maybe a dozen people or one ox. The boats owners had clearly organised themselves and whichever of them you spoke to the price was the same and always high. We had come across many on our journey who had been happy to help us out of kindness, but these rough men were not. They knew that we had no choice except to journey ever further up-river, and that with every passing day the threat posed by the advancing Romans became more real.

They were realistic though; they knew that we had little actual coin but that we did have tools and weapons, furs and pots, and these they could trade on for a tidy sum once the wave of disruption caused by the invasion had swept across them and the markets had returned to normal.

The price was set in negotiation by the Elders who by right had become the leaders of our band of refugees, and because they spoke for all of us, they were able to keep the crossing to a price that we all could manage.

And so, the following dawn, we made our way to the holding area where we were told to sit and wait. The waters looked calm enough and we were eager to be on our way, but the boatmen just smiled and waved us back and told us that we must wait for the passing of the tide. This confused me. I had seen the river below the Caburn back up, deepen and widen when the tide was high and the rivers flow reversed, but I did not think that that would be any cause for concern, indeed, it might even help the boatmen to steer their heavily laden vessels to the far bank. And then the tide arrived.

We heard it first. A sort of gurgling, rushing, rumbling noise that grew louder as the moments passed. Many of us stood and gazed downriver and so caught first sight of the wave of tumbling water that surged around the bend and swept towards us. But it was not a wave, it was a wall or even more like a step up, for as the rippling grey mass passed us, we saw that the water behind it was as high as the leading edge, which was soon vanishing around the next bend to our right. Now I understood why we had to wait for the tide. If that had caught us midstream, we would not have survived the impact.

Excited by what we had seen and by the prospect of leaving the lands of the Atrebates and entering the mountains and forests of the far west, we all scrambled down to the landing stages in small groups and climbed aboard. They had told us to stay well back so that there would be no danger during the loading. The boats strained against the flow and we were soon approaching the far bank.

It was then that the boatmen pulled their trick. The price that we had paid, they said, was the boarding price. There would be a second charge for the safe landing. This caused uproar, but short of seizing the unfamiliar oars in those dangerous waters, we had little choice and soon the crooked thieves had most of our decent pots and a large number of fine furs stacked behind them in the bows of the boat.

It was only then that they took us to the shore, and only then that we realised the cleverness of their ploy. That first crossing carried the warriors. When they had recommended that, they had said that we would need to be sure that the area was safe. That there were thieves and bandits waiting to prey on the unwary travellers. Now we realised that the women, the old, our children and the weak were still on the far bank, so any thought of taking back our goods was hopeless. If we did, we would have to navigate the swirling currents ourselves and none of us felt that we could.

So we had to stand well back from the shore as a condition of them bringing the rest across, with children held till last, since they could most easily be tossed overboard if we made a move back towards the landing place.

As the last boat approached the others stood off and a sudden array of bows appeared to make us stay clear, and so their job was done.

Even so, we were at least now in the lands of the mountain clans, and with two great rivers between us and any advancing Roman army, and for that at least, we were grateful.

Chapter 10

Into the Wild Woods

Once again, our Druid was well prepared. As soon as we were all clear of the river and it was certain that we could not retrieve our stolen goods, he led us almost due north. We could see the rising mountains to our left and hardly needed to be told that the range would be cut by fast flowing rivers heading south. So, even though it seemed like a diversion to be heading in the direction that we were we knew that once we reached the ridge that ran west across the top of the river valleys our progress would be swift.

I know that it made no sense, but it seemed to me the light was different this side of the great river. The colours were more intense, and everything just looked deeper. Maybe this was because if the frequent rain that swept in from the west washing everything clean, or maybe it was because Alane and I were spending more and more time in each other's company as our feelings deepened.

As we made our way north huge clouds rolled across the sky and the sun was often obscured to the point that it felt like dusk in the middle of the day. Wraiths of mist trailed through the dark green of the forests that soon surrounded us and it was easy to feel the presence of ancient powers. The fallen trees that we sat on when we rested were soft, so much so that I could push my fingers into them as if they were made of sand, causing a furious burst of activity from the beetles, centipedes and earwigs that dwelled in the decaying timber.

We saw no-one in those first days, but I had a constant sense that we were being watched from within the dark shadows of these trees that never shed their leaves and we all kept a constant vigil.

Eventually we turned into the west and the ground, littered with rocks and sudden streams, rose up into the rumbling storm clouds that seemed to be an eternal and unchanging part of this new world, but new only to us. Everything about it spoke of endless time and an eternity of nature's forces moulding the lands in which all of the people who came here, were guests.

Our efforts were rewarded when we reached a high plateau. There were still rugged peaks rising all around us, but we were now able to make faster progress across flat terrain strewn with gorse and scrubby trees that had all been bent in the same direction by the constant winds that swept in from the west.

Herds of wild horses paid us scant attention and the presence of tough looking sheep spoke to us of human settlement, but of those humans, for now, there was no other sign.

Even when it wasn't raining, which wasn't often, the air was full of damp mist and it crossed my mind that the weather and the landscape alone would discourage the Romans from coming here.

We camped in shallow depressions or in the lee of outcrops where we could, but they provided scant comfort with very little material to make fire or even the most basic of shelters. Our hunters would not pursue the horses, and we all decided that to take a sheep might provoke our as yet, invisible hosts.

It took some days to make our way across this high place but eventually we began to descend into a valley where the way was easier, and the trees provided more shelter. A river flowed down it and we followed that, keeping to the western bank, having crossed it as a narrow torrent further up.

Our Druid led us quietly on. Here there were signs of settlement, but not of the ramparted camps that we had been used to in in the south, and that we had passed many of along the way. These settlements had the feel of movement. They looked as if they could be struck in an hour if there was a need for the inhabitants to disappear into the deeper valleys and darker woods.

Ahead of us the valley narrowed into a gorge with steep cliffs and rough pinnacles around it. This was where the river made its way through the southern foothills before finding its way into the sea.

We had no doubt that a Roman legion could make its way through that unwelcoming gap, but they would be facing the possibility of attack from above as they came forward in a narrow column over uneven ground.

It was here that we found the ever-growing pool of people.

Many of them gathered to greet us as we straggled into the camp. We were presented with bread and cups of ale and guided to an open space large enough for us all to settle together. It felt like we had reached the end of our long journey and, in some ways at least, I suppose that we had.

The shelters were soon erected, and a safe hearth made. Our neighbours came over to talk and help and, over those first meals, we learned that many had arrived with stories much like our own. Some displaced directly by the advancing Romans, and many others made to leave by Britons who used the Roman's friendship to take what they wanted. Many had been robbed, many had become ill and fallen by the wayside. Some had died.

But there were stories also of kindness and comradeship, like mine when I spoke of how Macklyn and Olwen had taken me in and protected me and treated me as if I was their own.

We had other visitors in the days that followed. The Hill Tribesmen who were our new people. The owners of the hill sheep and Masters of these Mountains.

This land was theirs and had been since the oldest stories were first told. Their words were strange, and it became clear that we would need to learn their tongue, since this was where our future would unfold.

The Druids, it was clear, were to be the ones who made this happen. I had not realised, but they seemed to speak several tongues, unless they communicated by some other means.

It was through them that we discovered that these people had decided to abandon their hillforts on the low hills of the southern plain when news began to arrive of the Roman's attacks on the much larger forts in the east, and to take to the Black Mountains where they would be hard to find and even harder to fight.
Now they were waiting and preparing for the battles that they

knew lay ahead, but battles of a different sort to those already fought and lost. In these battles they would use the mist and the mountain ways and the dense woodland to strike and move and strike again, until the Romans either settled for the land they had already taken, gave up, or died.

They were organised and the men and boys would spend most of their days on the flat land by the river working on their fighting skills. I hoped very much that I would be able to join them soon.

Chapter 11

The Thirteen

We had been in the camp for several days before our Druid came to find me. Galvyn had been successful in fishing the new river and I was sitting by the fire gutting the catch and removing the scales and bones before adding the flesh to the simmering pot of vegetables.

He knelt next to me and stared into the flames for some time before speaking.

"I have come to take you to the place for which you have been searching".

I knew that he was talking about my oath to carry the three torcs to safety.

"Is it far?" I asked, already feeling a little sick in my belly at the thought of what I might find.

"It is not far. We will be there and back before night falls".

"Will I be safe?"

"You are safer than you can know. You have carried the torcs for many long passages of the moon, and for that, they will be grateful".

"Who are they?" I had to ask the question even though I sort of knew what he would say. Part of our growing was the story of the Druid Clan who lived in the Mountains of the West from whom the knowledge of all our Druids came.

"You know who they are. Come"

And so, he stood. I put down my knife and wiped my hands on an old cloth. The three torcs felt heavy now, even though I had gotten so used to them that they were like part of my skin.

We left the village on the hill-ward side and were soon climbing amongst outcrops of craggy limestone. He was right about the time that it would take, and I could still turn and see the camp in the valley below me when we stopped outside a black hole in the side of the hill.

Looking around, I noticed small piles of stones on which runes had been inscribed. I could see no pattern in their placement.

"What are these?" I asked.

“Offerings”, he replied, “for only a chosen few may pass into the darkness and so they leave their yearnings here, in the hope that their whispers will reach the chamber within and those who dwell there”.

“Am I of the chosen few?”

He looked down at me, his eyes shaded by his hood, and in answer took my arm and gently pulled me over the threshold of the darkness. The cold slapped my face and began to push its fingers into my clothing. Within a half a dozen paces there was no light at all in front of us and yet he moved as if he was strolling in a dappled woodland. I pulled back, without pulling away, and stood still. At first only our breathing filled my ears but, after a while, I could hear the faint sound of water falling. My guide took something out of his cloak.

“Stand still”, he commanded, as he knelt beside me.

I did. I could sense him kneeling next to me. Then I heard the strike of a flint on stone and the cave was, for a shining moment, blue and grey and rugged and the cold was only the cold. He struck again and I saw that he had caught the flame and set it into a small teardrop of reddish clay.

“This is a lamp”, he said, “I took it from a Roman camp. It will burn more steadily in the dark ways”.

We moved forward surrounded by the glow of the orange flame. Now I could see the rocks that were strewn across the floor and so I did not stumble. It was hard to judge but I felt that we were descending. I could feel the sharp mountain of rock above me and I was afraid.

“You do not need to fear”, he said, “this roof has been here since the Earth was young. It will not come down today”.

The sound of falling water grew louder step by step until, turning a corner sharper than the others we came out into a gaping chamber dressed in sweeping garments of white between fingers of rock pointing both up and down and which seemed to twist and slide as the lamp in the Druid’s hand moved from side to side.

On our left the source of the sounds now also came into view. A sheet of water pouring over a rocky shelf high on the side of this underworld and falling flat into a seething pool from which it fled through a narrow channel that cut the chamber in two before vanishing beneath the other rock face to our right.

We moved forward. He with confidence and me with an ever-increasing sense of dread. As we approached the tumult the freezing spray stung my skin and began to soak my tunic. We were close now to the inner edge of the falls and I could see that there was an even darker space behind it, the width of an arms span and the height of a tall man. Our Druid put a hand on my shoulder and held the lamp low so that I could see more clearly where I should put my feet. I reached out and touched the grey rocks, bracing myself physically as well as in my heart, and stepped into the gateway, for I assumed that that is what it must be.

The lamp was extinguished by the waterfall's misty breath and I had to feel my way forward. I realised that I was going up a narrow passage. I had taken only twenty paces or so when we emerged into the Heart of the Mountain Cave and I saw before me, lying flat upon a raised plinth, a quern stone through the centre of which flared a white fire the like of which I had never seen before. It drew me towards it and as I got closer each of the three torcs bound around my torso grew hot.

The brightness of the flame made the rest of the room seem darker, and it took me a moment to realise that we were not alone. Thirteen thrones carved of the sacred blue stone were spaced evenly around the flame, and in each of them a hooded figure sat motionless. Their eyes bright in the shadows.

When I realised that I was in the presence of the Mystery I stopped and stood as still as my beating heart would allow. Our Druid placed a hand on my arm and I knew that that was a signal. He was instructing me to unwrap the torcs and to place them on the quern. I loosened my tunic and carefully pulled out the cloth. He helped me to remove them safely and guided my hands to the quern, which I now saw was carved with intricate patterns that swirled around the fiery centre.

I was shaking with nervous anxiety as I recognised clear places in the dragon's form, for a dragon it clearly was, where the torcs should go. I took each in turn and put them in. Each of them seemed to open a channel in the beast and bright threads of light spun between them. Was this the blood in the dragon's veins spreading from its many hearts!

I stood back and so could see the whole of it. There were torcs other than those that I had brought. I counted nine, and even I could tell from the flow of the twisting light that there should be three more to make the dragon whole.

A collective sigh echoed around the hallowed chamber and, as one, the thirteen figures rose to their feet. The one who was directly in from of me raised his hands and pushed back the hood that had so completely shielded his face. He looked at our Druid, and then he looked at me.

"You have brought us a great treasure this day, Bran of the Caburn. These torcs were entrusted to the Island people many lifetimes since, when last the shadow of invasion flowed across the land. We wait only now for those from the North, and then the dragon will roar".

I did not know how to respond so I just stood in respectful silence, but I did feel pride that I had succeeded in completing the task set for me on that black night so full of sorry. Every day since then, when the sun set, I had turned away to look east wondering what had become of my mother and brothers and sisters. Those who I had asked had told me to give up hope, that there was nothing to be done, that by now they were more than likely already on the block in a slave market somewhere over the water and that the best I could hope for was that they were sold together to some kind man who would only use them as pack animals and at least treat them gently and feed them well. Even so, after a moment and when I had recovered myself a little, I could not help but ask.

"Sir. When I left the Caburn with these torcs my mother and

siblings were taken by the Romans who had destroyed it. I do not know if you can know but I can hope. Is it possible that your mystery can help me with mine? Can you see them in your white flame?" Again, a silence enveloped us, and I could hear my blood in my ears.

He did not ask in any way that I could tell of but the others now stood and they all took one step closer to the quern, all staring at its glowing heart. It seemed to me that a new brightness grew there and that the air was suddenly full of a low rolling, humming, strumming beat that rose and fell with my breathing. A time passed and the beating faded. He looked to me.

"We have done what we can. If the flame grants you knowledge in return for the torcs, it will come to you in a dream, and then you will know".

As one they all then turned. The flame slowly faded through blues and purples to black and before the Druid's lamp could return our sight, the thirteen were gone and we were alone in the cave. I looked at the quern. The torcs were there but now as much a part of the stone as any other, returned no doubt to their place in the earth.

I trembled as my friend led me carefully back through the outer cave until we reached the daylight. I could not speak, made dumb by the intense feelings aroused by the words that had been spoken in the sacred cave.

I could not wait for sleep and the dreams I knew that would come to me but because I was so excited, I knew also that sleep would not come easily to me, and so I went to Olwen.

"I must sleep tonight, I must". She sensed that I was about to reveal to her words that were meant for the cave only. She placed a finger on my lips to still them then brought to me a jug of warm mead. I drank it urgently. It was much stronger than the ale that we all drank every day, and it was not long before my lids became heavy and I drifted off into a honey scented otherness in search of my family.

And so it was that, that night, I ran with my brothers and teased my sisters and sat in the circle of my mother's arms. Then later, as if from a place above, I saw them when the General's Master of House came to select those that would serve on his estates in the Roman hills. I saw that this kind man chose families or young single men and women, and I knew that these enemies of ours had good in them as well.

When I woke, it was like waking many times and each time I lay in the same position, my limbs feeling warm and heavy and my heart eased by the certain knowledge that my birth family was safe from harm.

Chapter 12

The First Rite of Passage

Thankful for the understanding of my birth family's fate, given to me by the Druids in the Sacred Place, I found that I saw the present in a new and brighter light. I had not realised that my unresolved grief and nightmarish worries had been acting as an anchor to my emotions, constantly dragging me beneath the surface and into a world of isolation and numbness.

Now, when I opened my eyes and looked around, I saw Olwen, my mother, adding torn greens to the ever-bubbling pot. Macklyn, my father, now recovered so that you would not know how ill he had recently been. Galvyn, my little brother, restless with dreams under his twisted blanket, and Alane.

In that moment a new confusion entered my life, for the feelings I suddenly felt for her were not those of a brother for his sister. I saw her long nut-brown hair framing her oval face, her slim body flexing as she reached to left and right as she tended to the flat breads on the hot stones on the hearths edge and I knew that a new future had suddenly opened up in front of at least me and hopefully, in front of both of us. I stirred under my summer covering before sitting up and smiling at her. I was rewarded with a long moment when my eyes were lost in hers, then Galvyn jumped on my back, dug his fingers into my ribs and laughed at me as he pushed me over and sat astride my chest.

"You promised you would fish with me today!" he exclaimed. And so I had.

The river here in this season, was too narrow and fast flowing for coracles and so we spent the day fishing from the bank with lines. Galvyn's friends had all come along and it was pleasant to spend the time in boyish banter and fooling about. Even so I knew that something had changed and when we returned to our new shelter in the early evening my eyes sought first of all for Alane who, I saw, was looking directly at me. I handed her the fish. She took them with a shy smile and sat next to the flat rock that we used for gutting and cleaning whatever we had caught in the river or the forest.

After we had eaten, by some unspoken agreement, we both stood at the same moment and left to walk in the cool twilight. By some means my hand found hers and thus connected we entered into the trees.

In a clearing we stopped. I took her other hand in mine and we stood close. I closed my eyes, and we shared our first kiss.

After, we knew that our paths were now joined. That we would make a hearth together, have children together, and live our lives as one life.

Living as we did under the same roof with our parents, there were no mysteries about the adult world but even so, we knew the way of our people and that no act of creation could take place before the hearth stone had glowed red beneath our first meal as man and wife and so, with one more soft kiss, we made our way back to Macklyn, Olwen and Galvyn to share our news.

It was clear from their reaction that they were not surprised and also that they were very accepting. The sleeping places were carefully rearranged, with only Galvyn showing some mild annoyance at being pushed away from me, if only by an arm's length.

In the days that followed we were careful to include him on our walks and daily tasks and he was soon restored to his usually playful, sunny self.

Plans were made for our joining ceremony in the autumn, in the hope that the first child would then arrive in the spring.

But that was not the only change of that summer. Now that my thirteenth year was drawing to an end and I was showing signs of physical maturity, I knew that I would soon be called upon to begin my serious training to prepare me for membership of the warrior band.

The Western People were a united community, ruled from the High Hills by the One Prince and guided by the Oldest and Most Senior Druids but the threat posed by the advancing Roman army was very real. It would have been easy to dismiss it from the strength and safety of our Black Mountain stronghold, but we who had joined from the east had seen their power and efficiency and knew better.

It was a bright morning when I first came to the training ground. There were only a handful of boys my age in the camp, and only two of the girls had made the choice to train for war.

Owen was standing in the middle of the clearing. A young warrior of some twenty-five summers, he stood tall. He wore his reddish blond hair in a tight ponytail which fell to the middle of his lean torso. Tight swirling woad covered his right shoulder and spread down towards his stomach, showing that he had excelled in battle. His eyes were a deep blue.

We had heard of him and now he was here to train us.

"Welcome", he said, in a voice that made you want to please him. "Today you will begin a journey. At the end of that journey, you will be warriors. Not just because you will know how to fight. Not because you will be skilled in weapons but because you will know what it means to be honourable. Come now and we will begin".

There was no need for names. In a camp the size of ours it was an unwritten rule that we all learned the names of all the people. In this way no one could be tempted to behave badly and the children, known to all, could be kept safe.

I looked around hoping for a light chariot but there were none.

"Owen?" I asked, "I was hoping for chariots?"

Owen used his hand to indicate that we should sit. Once we were settled he began his first and perhaps on reflection, his most important lesson.

"Bran. From the stories you have told I think you know the answer before I begin. We are not fighting other Celts anymore. We are fighting the Romans now. They have no thought of honour for the foot soldiers. In their code it is the General who is applauded, even though he does not know the names of those who die to gain him victory. When you fight the Romans there can be no thought of calling on your ancestors or belittling theirs and there can be no thought of heroic demonstrations of skill before the fight is closed.

You saw when your father fell and your brother fell and your home was taken and given to the pet tribes of the coast that the Romans will stand as one behind their shield wall until you stray to close, bring you down like a pig, then step over you as you bleed to gain another two paces across the field. To fight the Romans, we need to learn a new way".

"What can we do?" As I asked the question, I could see the broken bodies of my father and brother and the others and I confess, the thought of another battle like that one did not fill me with fire.

"We will use our strengths and our advantages. The ramparts of this camp are only for animals not defence, and it is in the low valley rather than on the hill where we would normally build, so that we cannot be seen from far away. We live in tents not huts, so that we can quickly move, and there are manned beacons for a day's ride in all directions so we can never be taken by surprise. When we fight, we will use the same subtlety.

There will be no battles, only swift attacks from cover and distance. We will ride the mountain ponies, who are sure footed in this rocky land, and attack from hiding and from the high places.

We know that the Romans will come. They are greedy for the sacred gold and for the silver also but not so much for the land, in these hills at least. Our sting will make it too painful for them and they will take what they want and leave us alone".

When he had finished, we rose, and he led us up the slope to a corral of large branches which held a hand full of tough looking ponies. Stocky and shaggy. Broad backed and short in the leg. Each already had a simple arrangement of cords around its head to allow us to turn it left or right or bring it to a halt.

He jumped and swung his leg across the back of the largest one and dug in his heels behind its ribs which made it jump forward. Back and fore, he rode before us, showing us how to make the horse turn and stop. It looked like he and the horse were one creature so natural and easy were his movements. When he was done, he sprung back to the ground.

"Now choose a mount and do as I did. Drive it hard but also make it your friend. Feel the muscles twisting between your thighs. You will be horsemen before the day is done!"

I had never so much as sat upon a horse before. Our people used them for chariots and, when they were older, for drawing carts or sleds and there was already a knot of trepidation in my midriff. But I was determined and so I stepped forward and pushed my way towards a dappled pony that, I thought, was looking at me in a way that made me think that he was also choosing me, and so the lesson began.

I tried to jump and swing my leg as Owen had done and it mostly worked. At least, unlike some of the others, I did not over push and roll straight off again! When I had shuffled myself into a sort-of balanced place I dug my heals into the pony's flank, expecting a flying start to my career as a horseman, instead my mount just turned its head and looked at me then dropped its mouth to the ground and began chewing the tough mountain grass that it found there.

I look around clearly confused, and saw Owen watching me and smiling, but not in a way that caused me any offence. He kicked his horse into life and came along side me.

"You must show your pony your clear intention", he said, "push in the way that you wish to go at the same time as you dab it with your heals. Too hard and it will not work for you. Too soft and you will always be the boy sitting in the field on the chewing pony. Now try again".

And I did. The first time we went a few steps forward and stopped. The second, he bucked beneath me and I had to grasp his mane firmly to stop myself from falling but, after a good while but not so long as to be embarrassing, we were making fair progress together across the open slopes leading to the high places and I felt that I had at least begun my journey!

On another day we began our training with weapons. Once again Owen began by telling us the reasons why we must train in the way that we were.

"It is not just that the Roman soldiers do not seem to care much about their manly honour but only the honour of their Generals, they also have weapons made of an iron much harder than that which we have ever forged. When first we fought them we swung and blocked as we do when fighting other Celts. Careful with our footwork, caring how we looked almost as much as how well we fought. But we soon found that if we swing into a Romans sword and he blocks that swing, our blades will bend, or even snap, whilst theirs will not even show a nick upon their edges. For this reason, our smiths have been forging longer blades as sharp at the point as they can manage, and we have changed the way that we use them so that now we rush in and hold and stab and step away again.

So, now we will begin".

Owen pulled a skin off a large basket to reveal the bound handles of a bundle of swords. My heart first leapt but then sank, as I saw that they were wooden.

"Pick them up", said Owen, "and you will feel the cleverness".

I took a grip on one of the swords and pulled it free. Because I did not expect the weight the tip fell and for a moment, I used my other hand to hold it. The others were clearly having the same problem.

"To practice with wooden swords would be of some use but not much. Each of these has an iron core so that it has the weight of the swords that you will use when the time comes.

When you are trained enough the core will be taken out and beaten into your first blades, and for now you can use then with force and not kill each other!"

The knowledge that this wooden training sword had my first real sword at its heart gave a reality to the training, and I was keen to begin.

We were each paired with an older boy who was already familiar with the different ways that we could stand and move and parry and strike and soon the air was filled with the sound of wooden blades smacking into each other, although that lessened as we were encourages to tread more lightly and to strike with the point rather than the edge. Blunt though they were, wielded by the more experienced trainers they still hurt when they caught a bone, and I knew that I would be bruised beneath my tunic.

The days passed in this way and when we were able to ride our horses over rough ground without falling off and to hold our own in swordplay the next weapon was introduced. We were each given a lightweight bow and it was in the use of this that I found my skill. I had realised early on that I would never be more than a competent horseman and a solid swordsman, but I quickly became first good and later outstanding in the use of my bow.

To begin with we were stood in a line some distance from a copse of scrubby trees. Owen showed us how to fit the arrow, draw back the taut string, sight down the shaft and release it cleanly. After each round of five we then had to go and find the arrows that we had fired. At first this took a long time since many of them had missed the trunks and disappeared into the undergrowth, but the arrowheads were too precious to lose.

By the time that most of us young fighters had reached the point where they could hit the same point most of the time, I was already confident of a spread of less than a hands width and that felt good.

Next, we had to run across the face of the copse from side to side, only stopping to drop to one knee, quickly take aim and then fire our arrow. This was harder but not so hard as the final phase which was to fire our arrows from horseback whilst at a full gallop. Not only did this mean that we had to aim and fire whilst sitting on a bouncing rolling mount, but at the same time we had to control our pony with the muscles in our legs.

Moons came and went in this way. Eventually, all of our group were judged to be of a standard and the time came to blood us.

But first our wooden swords were to have their notched covers removed and the iron cores were to be beaten into our First Blades. That was the task of the smithy and each of us was to be a part of the process.

When my turn came, I carried my sword before me. He took it from me and with a few quick slices of his axe he removed the wood. Next, he placed the bar into the orange flames which I then turned blue by pumping on the leather bellows that fed into the clay base. When he judged it to be hot enough, he took hold of the outer end, his hand protected by a thick leather glove, and placed it on an anvil of hard rock. He handed me the hammer and I gave the iron its first few blows.

When it showed signs of changing shape, he took the hammer from me and thrust the bar back into the flames. Again, I pumped. When it was hot enough again, he took up the hammer and began to beat it and there, before my wide-eyed gaze, the blade was formed. Slowly and with much reheating, the long leaf shape became real and the metal took on the sheen of hardened iron.

When it was done and cooled, he gave me a whetstone and told me to find a quiet place to hone the edge before I took it to the wood worker and the leather man, who would make a hilt and bind it in.

Owen had said that there was a big difference between shooting at a tree and at a man whose life you were trying to take. We could not practise on men, but we could on the many wild boar that roamed the wooded valleys that fringed our Black Mountain hideaway and so, one cool and misty dawn, we mounted our ponies fully equipped for our expedition, said goodbye to our loved ones, and set off.

The plan was to cross the high ridge to the west and descend into the first of the five or so valleys that ran down towards the southern plain. There we would establish our base camp and begin our hunt. I remember still the first time I saw that view from the high pass. The spines of the land running away from us, the hazy plain beyond that, the great bay bound on the far side by a rolling peninsula, and the long grey-green mass on the far side of the wide channel that swept away from us on the right, leading to who knows what or where.

The summer was drifting towards the turning season and we were anxious to complete our training and return to our hearths, me more than the others I think, since Alane was waiting for me. Our plighting ceremony would take place on my return, so long as my face was marked with the blood of my first warrior kill.

Settlements were sparse in those valleys and we had no trouble finding a good site next to a fast-flowing stream with a rock face behind us, split by a narrow passage, that would allow us to escape should we be attacked. We did not fear the locals for they would mean us no harm, but we were always wary of the possible presence of the fast-moving Roman forces, even though I had not actually seen any sign of them since I escaped from their prison at the foot of the Caburn.

That first evening was spent around a small cooking fire made from dried wood and sheltered by the rocks to prevent our discovery. Guards were posted and changed three times and the night passed in storytelling and bravado, to cover our anxiety about the likely events of the next day.

Our military intention was not to defeat the Romans in open battle, we already knew that was simply beyond us and there was no point being foolish. It was our code that a warrior who rode into a battle he could not win was not brave, but selfish, and that there was no glory in suicide whilst there was in returning to your hearth having done all that reasonably could be done. Our tactical plan was to make the Romans decide that certain areas were not worth fighting for by causing casualties and confusion through hit and run attacks, mostly in woodland.

A swift assault from cover by fast moving horsemen who strike then run is hard to counter and arrows fired from the dark shade of a dense forest by a hidden archer would cause uncertainty and fear in even the hardest auxiliary. Our final training was to reflect all of this and so, at dawn, carrying only our weapons, we set off on the hunt.

The early morning mist seemed to writhe through the twisted branches of the ancient trees that grew larger as we descended. In looking for wild boar though, it was the undergrowth that was of more interest since it was in that that we would see the well-marked paths that the herd of boars that we already knew to inhabit the valley would follow. Our aim was to chase them into an open space where we could ride them down and use our bows to drop them.

Before the sun had cleared the boughs mid-way up the great oaks, we found the first path. It was well trodden and there were tufts of coarse brown hair snagged on bushes and brambles on either side. We rode in silence, we with our arrows and Owen with the great boar spear that needed a man's strength to hold it wedged against any charge a desperate boar might make.
My tummy was tight with anxiety as we made our way, scenting the wind as we did for the distinctive pungent smell that would tell us that the herd was nearby.

When it happened it happened very quickly. I saw the face of the boy in front react as the smell assaulted his nose, pulling back as if he had been hit and then, before any of us had time to prepare, the herd of boar crashed out of the dense undergrowth before us and headed straight down the path up which we had been following them. The lead boar split the legs of the first pony and, as he smashed through, he lifted his snout and twisted so that his polished tusks ripped into the inside upper legs on both sides. I had never heard a horse scream until that moment and the pain of it will stay with me forever. The horse reared and went over falling into the pigs that packed around their leader.

Luckily for it, and the boy who fell with it, the boars were intent on fleeing rather than fighting. By now I had drawn my sword and was able to hang low to my left. The lead boar had already passed me, but my blade did jar against the ribs of one that followed before skidding harmlessly off. I kicked in my heels and my pony jumped forward allowing me to reach down with my free hand and grab my fallen comrades outstretched arm and pull him clear.

Far from being the careful assault that we had hoped for, this was chaos. Boys were tumbling from their rearing mounts all around me and I was overwhelmed by the scent of blood and fear. And then they were gone, all but one, for Owen at the rear had had time to dismount and to brace his thick shafted spear against the base of a tree and to angle the lethal point and so the reckless charge of the great boar had ended with its forelegs dangling helpless as it bled out, the blunted point sticking out next to its rigid spine.

Allon, whose horse had been brought down, was squatting next to it holding its head still as best he could. The spilling blood had pooled around his knees. Allon had his sword in hand but there was no time to even give his pony the blessing of a quick end. The boar had ended his story before there was time for that.

Owen took charge of us, many of whom, me included, had tears on our cheeks. He helped us to gather our mounts and our possessions, then showed us how to gut the boar and tie it to a pole to sling between us, before pulling Allon on to the back of his much larger horse and riding him away. This to spare him the sight of us gutting and quartering his pony and preparing to carry it back, having carefully buried the entrails and other offal. We were not taking the meat to eat, horses had more dignity than that, but to make sure that we left no trace of our hunt for any wide-ranging scouts to find.

That night back at our camp, Owen spoke of the lessons that we should learn and of what we had learnt, just by going through the experience. It was fortunate, he said, that we had not been surprised by an enemy intent on killing us because if we had, we would all be dead, but that we should remember the smell of blood and the scent of death and be proud that we had helped each other when help was most needed.

"Tomorrow", he said, "we will hunt again and again the day after that, until it is the Boar who will be taken by surprise and we who will be triumphant!"

And so it was. A month passed in the wooded valleys of the southern slopes, and by the end of it we could move through the woods largely unheard and mostly unseen and there were fewer boar in the woods.

The day came to pack up our camp, bury the evidence of the campfire, dismantle the temporary smoke house and set off for the settlement where our families waited for us.

We sat proud on the backs of our mounts as we rode in. The guards had given word of our coming and the people had come out to meet us. I looked anxiously around for Alane but also for my brother and my parents, as Galvyn, Macklyn and Olwen had very much become. They were all there of course and as soon as was allowed to I broke away and rode towards them. Galvyn stretched up an arm and I hoisted him up behind me. The others walked alongside with Alane's hand in mine, until we reached our own hearth. I dismounted and held her in my arms, before hugging each of my parents.

I had made the journey into manhood and as a man, I could now join with my beloved and the next part of my life could begin.

Chapter 13

The Second Rite of Passage

The women gathered flowers to make garlands and the men cut branches for the bower. This was built in a clearing in the woods down by the river. Its floor was lined with bear skins, the hardest to get and therefore the most prized. The curved roof was threaded with the garlands. Around the doorway were the best pots that our community possessed filled with fruit and freshly caught and prepared fillets of fish.

On the morning of our day, Alane was taken by the women and I by the men. In private places our bodies were anointed with oils and carefully inscribed with the correct patterns in woad. The patterns that stretched across our back and arms were so placed that only when we embraced would they be complete. Our hair was braided into plaits, two that hung down our fronts, and a longer third one that bisected our backs.

In honour of my role as the torc bearer, we were given one each to wear. These were brought with great ceremony out of the mouth of the cave by our Druid. The True Elders never appeared; it would not have been right.

When the sun was at its highest, we each walked at the head of our own processions to the nearby grove where the greatest of Oaks of our valley stood. Its branches had been hung with garlands. Between these wind chimes of copper and bronze spun randomly catching the sunlight that filtered down through the green canopy. Our progress was marked by the beating of hide drums and children ran around us in excited circles.

When we entered the grove the drumming stopped, the children fell back, and we were both led to the centre. Because I had no blood parents with me, Macklyn stood for me and Olwen for Alane.

At the right moment. The Druid joined us by touching each of the torcs as he intoned the blessings in the ancient tongue. Macklyn then took my hand as Olwen took Alane's and placed them together. Fingertips first we slowly followed the curves of our palms until we gripped each other by our wrists.

Our parents stood back, the Druid bowed his head and withdrew a few paces, all present took a deep breath, raised their arms and thumped their closed fists to their chests, exhaling as one and the ceremony was done.

I placed my arm around Alane, our woad markings completing

each other and then we walked together to our bower as the others looked on with smiles of love and hope on their faces and in their eyes.

And so, we were together.

The following morning, we emerged to begin our new lives. Hand in hand we walked back to the family hearth. Macklyn, Olwen and Galvyn were there to greet us with a rich breakfast of smoked meats and fish and rich creamy cheese washed down with cool ale to mark our first day.

When we had eaten, Macklyn pulled back the skin that covered the dwelling to show us that the interior had been rearranged so that we had our own space in which to lie together, which was raised by thick furs and covered in a deep woollen blanket. We hugged them all in thanks then Alane sat with Olwen at the hearth, whilst Galvyn and I went to catch some fish for our meal later in the day.

Chapter 14

Caractacus

I heard the strumming of hooves long before I saw the first rider.

I was sitting at the open hearth in front of our dwelling. My hands were covered in wet clay from the coils that I had been rolling in preparation for making a storage jar that Olwen needed for the stewing of the summer fruits.

Moments later, the hoard of Horsemen rode out of the woodland and into our camp. No alarm had been raised and we knew that we had only friends nearby and so we were more interested than worried. There must have been fifty or more in that first group. Later I learnt that there were several hundred nearby.

In the forefront was a man of great height on the biggest horse that I had ever seen. My eyes were drawn to the torc around his neck. Naked to the waist his muscular torso was a mass of woad swirls and I knew that there was only one man that this could be, and I was right.

Caractacus, the warrior Prince who was leading the resistance against the Roman invasion. I stood out of respect, as did all the others as he rode by.

The warriors behind him were almost as impressive. Tough looking men with the scars of battle cut into them. Each arrayed with weapons of every sort.

When the last had past, I followed them up the slope, but I did not get too close. Even as I approached Caractacus swung himself off his mount and strode into the mouth of the dark cave that led to the Druids Chamber, whilst the others dismounted more conventionally and stretched or sat around. I went back to collect a bowl of stew and returned to hand it to a warrior on the edge of the group. He smiled as he took it then offered me his hand. We gripped wrist to wrist in the way of fighting men and I swelled with pride that he, in extending such a gesture, was recognising me as a man to respect. Whilst he began to eat, I squatted next to him.

"I am Bran".

At that he looked quickly up, his knife blade paused halfway between bowl and mouth.

"Bran of the Caburn", he asked, "Bran the bearer of the Southern Torcs?"

“Yes”, I answered simply, “I am that Bran”.

“Then Raven, I am a proud man to be eating with you. We had heard of your journey”.

“It was not so hard. I was travelling with my new family and fell in with good company who eased our way”.

“There were others also who eased your way. Caractacus, our Prince, knew of your endeavour and sent many to harry the Romans as they made way behind you. Without that you might have been caught. Also, when that Druid found us and told us of your trials, Caractacus sent word to the Atrebates to open the way”.

“I did not know”.

We were silent for a while, then I spoke again”.

“How are you known?”

“I am Sloan, of the Prince’s Guard”.

“Why is Caractacus called Prince and not King?”

"There can be no King over the Celts until the thirteenth ring is complete. You, Torc Bearer, would have seen the fire in the rock, the gold-maker. There must be twelve around the flame to complete the thirteenth. Only then will our lands be safe and only then can our Prince be crowned as King".

"There were nine, with the three that I carried".

"You carried the three rings of the South. Gathered at Caburn by the Druids after the first invasions. Caractacus gathered the Mid Land rings years ago, but we wait still for the rings from the North".

"Are they coming?"

"Two of them are known to be on their way. Each on a separate journey. That is why we are here now, to see if they have arrived or been heard of. The third is missing. Last seen on the largest of the islands furthest to the north, before the Wild Lands begin".

"What will Caractacus do? If the Last Torc cannot be found?"

"The time of hope is getting ever shorter. The Romans are moving swiftly across the Celt lands. Nothing we have done has made any difference by more than a few days. We have one Great

Fort left and that is where Caractacus will make his last stand. If we must die, then we will die with honour in a High Place, behind the last ditch."

"But Owen says that we must change our ways. He says that there is no honour in throwing yourself on to a hard sword when you can defeat your enemy with a sharp arrow point from the safety of the trees".

"Ah, yes. But Owen is not a Prince. Princes do not think in the ways of ordinary men".

"Will you go with him?"

"I will go with him. I have followed him since I was a boy. I will follow him now, even to death. Who knows? Perhaps the Roman General will think that each Fort so defended is too high a price to pay for the Mountain lands beyond and turn away".

There was a commotion in the entrance of the cave. Moments later Caractacus strode out. His gait was strong and brave. His shoulders those of a warrior, but his face held something dark, a shadow maybe of the events to come.

He swung himself into his saddle and his troop took this as their signal to do the same. I quickly stepped away from the twisting mounts and watched as they rode down the slope into the centre of the settlement. There Caractacus stopped, raised himself up and looked around. The Elders had gathered there in honour of the Prince, whose voice was all that you would expect it to be.

“We go”, he said, “to face the Romans in a great fight. There will be honour for those who stand with us on that day. Their names will be spoken of in awe. I call upon your warriors to gather their weapons and join us, but only those of proper age and not yet with wife or child”. None went.

Those last words told what he already knew, and what twelve months later we heard to be true from a ragged group of survivors who rode with no swagger into that same open space.

They told how Caractacus, Prince, gathered a great force in a High place and how they fought like angry bears to defend their land and of how they were overwhelmed at the last ditch and taken, cheated of a proud death, and were now gone from us to who knows where beyond the narrow sea.

Perhaps, I thought, he will end up where my birth family is and that will connect us in some little way again, as we are connected when we both look up at the same moon however far apart we may be.

Perhaps he will tell my mother the story of the Torc Bearer from the South and she will know that I am safe. If only I could know that she was. But I cannot and I must carry that grief with me wherever my fates take me.

Chapter 15

New Life for Old

Autumn turned quickly into Winter. In these high places that meant snow at best and driving sleet at worst. The only benefit being that the Romans would have set up their wooden forts and encamped until the weather improved and the next campaigning season could begin. We fixed the coverings of our shelters with large rocks and kept an eye on the level of the river, although it was fast flowing in our valley and there was no real risk of flooding for us.

My beautiful Alane was with child and in the smoky confines of our dwelling, she grew larger almost daily. Her skin glowed and her hair shone, and I loved her even more, risking the rains more than once each day to go and find her fresh meat and fish to add to the supplies that we had stored for the winter.

Each evening we sat and listened to the stories, my hand resting on her tummy above our unborn child. Some of those tales were of the earlier parts of our lives, some the stories of our ancestors, near or distant, and some just pulled from the smoke to entertain.

The baby came, as it should, with the spring. The custom meant that no man could witness that beginning and so I spent the anxious hours wandering the riverbank with Galvyn, waiting for the new life to join us. Our son was born with the rising moon, a good omen. Healthy and strong and clear of eye. We called him Briann, since he was a man born of the hills and it was in the hills that he was destined to live out his life.

It was during these months that our joyed was tinged with tears and sadness, as it became clear to us that Macklyn was fading from our world.

In the fall it was he who would tell the best stories, full of careful detail, his voice rich and respectful, but as the winter set in he became more listener than teller. He moved less and when he did his joints were stiff or even locked and he would need my arm to pull himself up, which was different to being pulled up by me.

As each moon came and passed, he slept more and ate less, and we all knew that his time was near.

And then one morning Olwen woke to find him gone. His breath stilled and his frail old body cooling next to her. But that is a good death and his had been a long life, given meaning by his love and kindness.

The people gathered at our door and came in turn to touch his chest and forehead and to give him their words. Our Druid, who spent all of his time now deep in the mountain, came with his woad to mark the corpse with the signs of family, tribe and respect.

We slept together that night and then, as the watery sun pulled itself over the ridge, Galvyn and I took our ox blade and antler picks and dug the round hole high up on the slope near the dark shadows of the cave entrance. We knew to choose a bank where the earth was deep enough and not bound by roots. We did not want to use one of the old grain pits. For Macklyn, so far from his life-home, it did not feel right, and we wanted him to be in a high place where he could feel the sun and see to the far places.

When we were done, Olwen and Alane joined us with the baby. Our tears flowed easily, and we let them seed the earth where Macklyn would lay.

An honour guard of young warriors who had placed Macklyn on a settle, now carried him out of his here home and brought him at shoulder height, to his grave.

They laid the settle down and two druids came to prepare him finally. One knelt at his shoulders and the other took hold of his ankles. Gently they pushed and Macklyn folded at the waist into the womb shape.

When he was ready, we, his family, lifted him gently and lowered him into the pit. We placed him so that his head was to the north and his face towards his home in the lee of the southern downs. Each of us then cut a lock of our hair and placed them on his chest, close to his heart.

In honour, the older of the Druids took out a bag of gold shavings created when the Torcs were made and dusted them across him.

We all stood a while in our own silent place and thought of him. Of all that he had meant to us and of all that he had done for us.

Finally, family first, everyone came and placed a scooped handful of earth to cover him, and soon it was done and Macklyn was gone from us in the here and now.

Chapter 16

When the Romans Came

In the weeks after the passing of Macklyn the flowers began to bloom, the trees bud and the skies were huge and blue.

News came of the Romans stirring and, with the thirteenth ring incomplete, we knew that it was only a matter of time before the Legions began to thread their way onto the Southern Plains where they would find grain and slaves and in through the valleys of the north where they would find gold.

Owen gathered in the warriors and the weapon makers spent their days sharpening swords and honing spearheads. Not all of these were iron. The knowledge of bronze working, and even flint knapping was still common, and we all knew that we would need every weapon available to us.

The beacons were checked and manned and groups of us were sent out to roam the ridges and the valleys to watch and wait.

It was on such an expedition that I found myself riding in the surf on the long beach where the waves rolled in relentlessly from the endless blue of the ocean and I was minded once again of the fate of my mother and my younger brothers and sisters, who had stood in the surf of the south coast with me, beneath the white cliffs of the haven in those simple days before the Romans came. It was at times like that, that even my new family and all the love we had could not protect me and the tears would flow again.

Later we rode up the steep slopes of the ridge that divided the valley. At the top we dismounted and ate a simple lunch, casting our eyes across the water to the hills in the south and around to those that pushed out from the mainland into the mouth of the ocean. There seemed to be so much land, and with only a scattering of thin whisps of smoke from hearth fires.

When I turned my back on this view and looked back along the ridge, I saw the stronger columns that meant that the beacons were lit, and beyond those the roiling black smoke of a burning settlement, and I knew that the Romans were coming once again.

We quickly made ready and rode swiftly towards the foothills, aware that we did not want to find ourselves between the advancing Romans and the sea.

That night we made a cold camp and ate dried meats. Owen was busy talking to each of us in turn to make sure that we understood what we were to do should we encounter a main

Roman force. His message was simple, run. Run back to the hills and try to gather in the safe places.

Our time would come he said, when we drew the Romans into the wooded valleys where we knew the paths and they did not. Our only chance, he reminded us, was to convince the Commanders that the price they would have to pay for our poor land was too high.

And so it was that seven nights later, we found ourselves in a well concealed clearing off to the side of the most obvious trail up into the largest valley running north off the plains. It was not the most obvious because it was the most used, but because we had made it so by the careful cutting back of branches and stamping down of the undergrowth beneath the tough hooves of our mountain ponies.

Our men down the way signalled to us with arrows fired one to the other, tied with coloured threads to tell us how far away the Romans were. I could taste metal and felt strange and distant. My mouth was dry, so I took a swig from my leather flask.

And then I heard the first sounds of men moving along who were wearing armour. They did not speak, such was their training, even though they could not have been expecting to encounter us so soon since their scouts lay dead, piled together under a nearby Oak.

As the first of them passed a tide of anger began to rise in me. Images of the burning Caburn came to mind. Pictures of my father and brother lying dead at the feet of indifferent auxiliaries. Of my mother and my brothers and sisters bound and alone and headed for who knows what treatment at the fate of their captors. And of Alane and my child, and Olwen and Galvyn waiting in our new home for the outcome of the fighting of these few days, and I knew that I was ready.

The stream of men seemed to have no end. It ran on upwards, the sunlight striking and skittering off helms and breastplates as, soon, our arrows would.

And then the moment came. Owen raised his arm in a silent signal. The tension passed through us like a wind. We sat taller and gripped our bows more tightly. I could hear my own breathing and was suddenly bathed in cold sweat. Then he kicked his horse forward and we followed down the paths that we had cleared the day before.

We released the first salvo of arrows as we burst through the last of the cover aiming always for the face or knee, the points where the Roman armour was least strong, and many fell. For once the famed Roman discipline deserted the beleaguered troops and the line broke as each man fled to try and save himself.

The Commanders at the front of the column were so far away that they would have been barely aware of our attack, even so, we knew that the day would be ours only if we struck and ran before our enemies could gather themselves.

Another two quick clouds of arrows followed the first and then we were amongst them. Scattered as they were, they were weak, vulnerable to the narrow stabbing blades with which we now attacked them. I gave no thought to how they had come to be here. To whether they were soldiers of Rome herself, or prisoners given the choice to fight or die in the galleys or the mines. In this moment they were just men who threatened my family and my land and who had driven me from my home and taken my father and brothers lives and stolen my mother and little brothers and sisters from me, and so I was able to do what must be done. And so I did.

It was only later, in my dreams that the panicked eyes would haunt me, and the smell of their fear fill my nostrils and I would weep for them as their loved ones would weep.

It was only a few short moments before we were through them and crashing into the deep woods on the other side of the narrow pass.

Our escape route had long since been planned and by the time the Romans had turned and formed their lines and squares, we were gone, heading for the ridge and the safety of the Black Mountains beyond.

Epilogue

We had lost no-one in the attack, although some were wounded, mostly in the legs, so when we rode back into our village there was no hint of sadness to taint our victory.

Certain of our safety because our network of lookouts and beacons was securely in place, we built our fire high and feasted on deer and pig. One of the pits was breached and fresh ale flowed, with berry wine in leather flasks passed from hand to hand in friendship and salutation. Galvyn had his first real taste of this that night as he was now approaching manhood, and so was carried over my shoulder to his bed not much after the sun had set and the blue moon had taken its place low on the sharp horizon.

Next day the ashes of the fire smouldered sending thin wisps of grey smoke twisting painfully into the wind. Lumps of discarded meat on gnawed bones were being chewed by thin dogs. Galvyn sat up holding his head and asking for cool water, which Olwen gave him with a bowl of plain porridge.

I stepped out into the cold of early morning in the mountains and looked instinctively up to where Macklyn was buried near the dark cave.

Dark figures stood there, motionless. The Druids faces were shaded by their hoods and they were remarkable in their stillness. They all looked to the south and so I turned to follow their gaze.

A distant beacon burned against a red sky.

The End.

Also by Gareth Jones

Non-Fiction

On This Day for Teachers

Saving the Planet, one step at a time {as "Plays in the Rain"}

Dealer's Choice, The Home Poker Game Handbook

Mametz Wood, Three Stories of Wales {First published by Bretwalda}

Outstanding School Trip Leadership

Top Teacher Tips for Outstanding Behaviour for Learning {as Gethin James}

Cheeky Elf Solutions for Busy Parents

A Short Report on the Planet known locally as Earth {as Abel Star}

Make Your Own Teepee

Travelling with Children {First published by Bretwalda. Now in its second edition and fully illustrated}

Identifying Gifted and Talented Children, and what to do next

Outstanding Transition, A Teacher's Guide

An Unofficial set of revision notes for the Edexcel GCSE, History B, American West

An Unofficial set of revision notes for the Edexcel GCSE, History B, Medicine Unit

The Big Activity Book for KS3 Drama {published by ZigZag}

The Drama Handbook KS2 {this is an age adapted version of the above. They should not be bought together}
Personal Learning Project Guide {March 2020}
The Tower of Hanoi {The 127 Solution}

Short Stories

The Christmas Owls {Based on an idea by Millie C}
The Pheasant that Refused to Fly {includes “The Cave.” Winner of the 2018 Hailsham Arts Festival Short Story Competition}
The Unicorns of Moons Hill and the Broken Heart {Based on an idea by Millie C}
An Owl called Moonlight and The Midnight Tree {Based on an idea by Millie C}
The Amazing Adventures of Edwina Elf {Based on an idea by Millie C}
A Mermacorn Christmas Adventure {Based on an idea by Millie C}
“A Shirt for Mr De Niro” and other Stories
Hailsham Festival Anthology 2019 {Edited by}
Hailsham Festival Anthology 2020 {Edited by}
Mollie’s Midnight Adventure with the Magical Moon Magician
The Valley of the Rainbows

Plays

Georgina and the Dragon {First published by Schoolplay}

Jason and the Astronauts {Also first published by Schoolplay}

Pelias Strikes Back! {The sequel to Jason}

William Shakespeare's Romeo and Juliet, A new adaption for KS2 and KS3

Dr Milo's Experiment

GET SANTA! From the original East Sussex film project

The Space Pirate Panto

Cinderella and the Raiders of the Lost Slipper {includes "Goldilocks", the full story}

William Tell, The Panto

Novels

Heartsong

Get Santa: The Novel

Undefinable

Short Stories and Plot Outlines that would make GREAT FILMS, Mr Steven Spielberg, Sir

Quick Comedy Sketches for Young Comedians {as performed at "The Paragon Spectacular, White Rock Theatre, Hastings}

The Quiz That Keeps on Giving. A Charity Fund Raiser

JPR Williams X-Rayed my Head

Printed in Great Britain
by Amazon